Swimming
and other stories

Bernard Steeds

2024

laieta press

Swimming and other stories

Laieta Press

Wellington

New Zealand

ISBN 978-1-0670384-4-1 (print edition)

ISBN 978-1-0670384-3-4 (kindle edition)

A catalogue record of this book is available at the National Library of New Zealand.

Swimming

and other stories

Acknowledgements

'The Sea as Past' won the *Sunday Star-Times* short story prize in 1988 and has been broadcast on Radio New Zealand.

It has also appeared in *Sunday 22: The Winners of the Sunday Star-Times Short Story Competition* (2006) and *The Penguin Book of Contemporary New Zealand Short Stories* (2009).

'Ice' was shortlisted for the Sunday Star-Times short story prize in 2000 and was broadcast on Radio New Zealand.

'It gets cold up here' was first published in *Boys' Own Stories: Short Stories by New Zealand Men* (2000) and was broadcast on Radio New Zealand.

Earlier versions of these stories appeared in the collection *Water* (Penguin Books New Zealand, 2001).

Cover design and illustration: Ursula Palmer Steeds

Contents

Swimming

Benjamin wakes early, before first light, before the air has lost its chill or its hush, and lies for a moment in this pre-dawn quiet, trying to recall a dream, something gauzy, something faint, a colour, a field of red. The memory slips and fades, sinking beneath waves of morning thoughts—his aching body, his plans for the day, the familiar scent of his wife, Juliet, lying beside him, breathing softly, her eyes closed and still. He reaches across, touches her shoulder.

'Petal,' he whispers. 'It's time.'

She stirs, mumbles, and he tries again, prodding this time. She opens her eyes, looks at him accusingly.

'What?' she says.

'It's time.'

'Already? I've barely slept.'

'Already,' he says.

'Christ,' she says.

She shakes her head, pushes back the covers, and slowly swings her legs to the floor. He watches as she crosses the room, hand cupped against her hip, forming a brace. She goes into the bathroom, turns on the shower, and the water pitters on the porcelain and steam seeps into the bedroom through the open door. He watches, breathes its scent, then turns to look out the window, into the rising blue light. He can just make out a faint line of clouds floating behind the tops of trees.

After a few minutes Juliet emerges, moving more comfortably. He lies back, examines her: hair, normally a round, white swirl like a snow-freeze, now matted, turned silver and limp by the shower; forehead, pronounced, intelligent; nose, on the long side, symmetrical; mouth, terse; chin, a tiny scoop that slides towards the greying pouches of her neck; shoulders, round but muscular; breasts, small; ribs, faint sand-ripple shadows; belly, the slightest, most beautiful of paunches, puckered at the belly-button; hips, smooth curving lines, like wishbones... She steps into her swimming costume and pulls it up, covering herself in a field of fading pink roses.

'Your turn,' she says. Benjamin hauls himself up from the bed, stands unsteadily. His knee wants to give way. He takes a few tentative steps, stops, tests the joint. When he can move again he goes to the bathroom, removes his pyjamas, steps into the still-running shower. It is, as always, too hot. He turns it down and for the next few minutes soaps himself and uses a flannel to clean his skin. He sings to himself, softly, After you've gone and left me crying, after you've gone there's no denying...

When he has finished, he steps out and dries himself in the bedroom. Juliet, now in a plain sundress, watches him put on his blue swimming shorts, his brown cotton trousers, his pale blue shirt. They take the elevator to the ground floor and walk, hand in hand, out into the rising light. They cross the park and continue past the docks where cruise liners berth, along a promenade which curves languorously under seaside cliffs, to a small, grey beach. At this time of the morning no-one else is around. The sea is glassy and reflects pink petals of sun and white lights from buildings across the bay. They strip off their clothes. He looks at her, raises his palms questioningly. She takes the first step, slow and solemn, flamenco-style, into the glassy water. Its surface divides and heals behind her as she arches her back, kicks her legs and swims away gracefully, trailing silver hair.

Benjamin counts: fifty-nine, fifty-eight, fifty-seven, fifty-six, fifty-five, fifty-four, fifty-three, fifty-two... and exactly one minute after Juliet he runs, knees high, into the water, breaking its surface with a bellyflop. They swim beyond the curve of the beach, along a line of rocks, through the blue-black depths, to an island that rises, glistening and bush-green, in the middle of the harbour.

'The water is nice today,' Benjamin says, as he hoists himself on to the island's wooden pier.

'Yes,' says Juliet. 'It's softer than usual.'

They sit for a few minutes, under a bright sky, before Juliet dives back into the water and skims along, just beneath the waves. When she has been gone for exactly a minute she stops, turns, raises her head, calls out 'Catch me!'

Benjamin pulls air into his lungs, flexes his legs and dives in from the pier, causing a great wave to ripple across the sea. He cuts the water with his hands, displaces the ocean with his kicking thighs, forces his searing limbs to move faster, faster, faster. But when he reaches the beach she is waiting. Water falls from her in a shroud. Shining droplets pool at her feet. Benjamin takes her towel and pats her hair until it is almost dry, then he pushes it aside and kisses the freckles on her neck. She embraces him, allowing her hands to move over his back.

'I love you,' she whispers.

In unison, as if it is rehearsed, they flick their towels open and lay them on the sand. Benjamin's knee gives way as he sits down. Juliet cups a hand against her hip.

'We're like penguins,' Juliet says. 'In the ocean we make sense. On land we waddle.'

Benjamin gazes out to the sea. 'It's not us,' he says. 'Time's to blame.'

When he turns to Juliet she has a hand over her face, shielding her eyes from the sun. She looks as if she needs to sleep.

'I suppose we've got old,' he says.

When she doesn't answer, he turns back towards the sea and watches its movements—the ships and ferries entering the harbour, the dinghies and sailboards closer to shore, the water itself, rising and falling slowly, its surface speckled with bright crescents of reflected sun.

Later, after they have returned to their apartment and put on fresh clothes, they walk back along the promenade to their favourite café. Juliet is pensive and Benjamin tries to cheer her up with jokes, but she seems not to hear him—she stares at her food, prods it around the plate. After a while she looks up and motions towards the beach.

'When I go,' she says, 'I want to be scattered there.'

Benjamin's eyes fill with tears. He wipes them on the back of his sleeve and looks away from her. She offers him a handkerchief.

'I'm just being practical,' she whispers. 'I don't want to be buried. I couldn't bear it. I'd suffocate. I want to be at sea.'

'No,' he says, raising a hand.

'No?'

'You won't go,' he says.

She laughs. 'I've been thinking about these things,' she says. 'As one gets older it pays to. I will go. You know I will.'

They finish the meal in silence, but afterwards, as they walk beside the marina, He holds her hand very tightly.

That night, as they sit together in the living room of their apartment, he asks, 'Did you mean what you were saying today?'

'Yes,' Juliet says. 'Do I ever say anything I don't mean?'

He is lying back on a sofa which faces the window. The night sky is blue and starless.

'You know I'll go first,' he says. 'I'll insist on it.'

She sits opposite him, in an easy chair. Between them is a table, on which sits a backgammon board, permanently set up for play.

'You can't know that,' she says, picking up a die and tossing it. Benjamin watches it roll across the board and come to rest with its six-side facing up.

'I can,' he says. 'I'll make sure.'

'No! You mustn't!'

'Then we'll go together,' he says, taking his throw. Another six.

'Who will scatter us?' she asks.

'We won't be scattered. We'll be buried at sea, in a glass casket, and we'll spend eternity watching the fish go by.'

She asks if he believes it, and he says 'yes'.

'You don't,' she says. 'I know you.'

'I do. I believe in the fish.'

'Benjamin!'

'Okay,' he says. 'If you want me to be serious, I don't believe in anything.' He tosses the die in the air. It strikes the ceiling and bounces against the windowpane. Juliet turns sharply. The glass is intact. When she turns back towards him, frowning, he says: 'Except you.'

That night, he dreams that he is diving in the deep black of the ocean. He feels something brush against his body and realises he is surrounded by squid. They have billowing bodies and long, stringy tentacles trailing behind them. Each gives off its own phosphorescent light: some green, some yellow. They float past him, their tentacles feathery on his skin. Eventually, only one is left. It is the smallest, and gives off the faintest light, a pale, greyish-green, which slowly fades out.

In the morning, before first light, he wakes Juliet by touching her hand as it lies on the bedclothes. They take turns at showering and dressing, and together they walk along the promenade and swim to the island and back. They have lunch at their favourite café, and in the afternoon they rest and read books about life in the ocean depths. In the evening, they sit together in the living room of their apartment, playing board games as the light outside fades. Days add up to weeks , weeks add up to months, all passing in much the same way. Their routine is interrupted only once, for five days in August, when their daughter Hannah visits from London—they shorten their morning swims, and spend longer walking on the promenade, and at night they abandon backgammon and sit around the table, looking at photographs, comparing memories. On the night Hannah leaves they cannot play backgammon because Juliet cries so hard she can't see the pieces, and in the morning, when Benjamin says 'It's time', she doesn't wake immediately. He props himself on a pillow and uses his free hand to stroke her hair and massage the pale lines of her face. When, at last, she opens her eyes, he tells her to rest. 'Don't get up now,' he says. 'It's only a swim. There's no need to get up. Not now.'

She brings her hand up and pinches herself between the eyes.

'It's just a little headache,' she says, as she turns back the covers. 'I'll be fine in a minute.'

'No,' he says. 'You're ill. I can tell. I can always tell before you.'

'You make things up,' she says. 'I've never been ill in my life.'

'Have so,' he says.

'Have not.'

She climbs from the bed and walks towards the bathroom. After a few steps she slumps to the floor. Benjamin is beside her in a second

'Juliet?' he pleads. 'What's wrong?'

He checks her pulse, which is weak.

'Please,' he says, 'say something!'

He cups his hands under her back and turns her on her side.

'I'm going to get my phone,' he says, 'and when I come back, I'll count to three and you'll wake and tell me what you've been dreaming.'

He leaves the room backwards, not daring to take his eyes from her. When he reaches the phone he dials 111 and asks for an ambulance. 'I don't know what she's doing,' he says.

Back in the bedroom, he lies beside her. 'It's going to be all right,' he whispers in her ear. 'It's going to be fine. I promise you that. It's all right. It's fine. I promise, I promise.'

When the knock comes at the door, he springs to his feet and runs to answer, wishing he had remembered to leave it open. He travels with her in the ambulance. When they reach the hospital, she is taken away and for two hours he waits in a corridor, staring at the blue linoleum floor, the faded woodgrain walls.

Whenever anyone comes near he looks up expectantly. A surgeon walks past. An intern wheels an empty bed. Two nurses stop in a doorway beside him, gossiping. A faint breeze stirs, though there are no windows; and the lights, every so often, flicker without quite going out. Eventually a nurse comes and asks his name. He has to think.

'Juliet?' he says.

The nurse leads him to a room where Juliet lies on a chrome-framed bed, with a thin blanket over her.

'Are you the husband?' a man says, approaching.

Benjamin nods.

'Your wife has had quite a serious stroke,' the man says. 'She's in a very deep sleep. I'm afraid it's impossible to say what will happen. We'll do everything we can to make sure she is comfortable, and we'll see how things go.'

When the doctor has finished, Benjamin takes him by the arm and leads him to the door.

'Please,' he says, 'if you can't bring her back, just leave us alone.'

He turns back towards Juliet. Her hair is spread about her in a silver halo, her skin translucent. He pulls up a chair and sits beside her.

'I don't know if you can hear me,' he says, 'but I will speak as if you can. I won't live without you.'

A sob rises from deep in his belly. To save her from hearing, he brings his fist to his mouth and bites. A trickle of blood runs from his knuckles. He pulls a handkerchief from his pocket and wraps the hand.

'Don't listen to me,' he says. 'Don't listen to the silly old fool. Just rest. Lie back and rest. Be comfortable. Rest, and it will be all right.'

He sits with her for hours, as the pale light from the window behind him fades.

'When we get out of this place,' he says, 'I will take you to Paris. We will swim down the Seine wearing striped swimming trunks that stretch to our knees. From Paris, we will head out into the countryside, past the golden palace of Versailles, through Fontainebleau and Dijon. We will swim in Champagne until we are a little tipsy, then make our way upstream, across a mountain pass, to Cologne.

'From the Rhine,' he continues, 'it is a left turn into the Main, then right at the fork into the Danube, which is brown, not blue as they say. We will swim upstream for a few hundred kilometres, and then, my love, we will crawl through canals and drainage ditches, until one of them spills us safely into the grey, lapping waves of Constance.'

He gets up from his chair and goes to the window. In the twilight of the street below, a traffic light changes from red to green, but there are no cars.

When he turns back to the bed, Juliet is just the same. Still, silent. He leans over and kisses her forehead. Her skin is dry and papery. He wonders how many times he has kissed her before—in the morning, before he is fully awake, or in the evening, when he is weary and unthinking— assuming she will always be there.

Soon, he drifts into sleep.

In the morning, a nurse brings him a breakfast of cornflakes and tea. She suggests he go for a walk, and promises to sit with Juliet until he returns.

The day is grey. A breeze blows and the leaves on some nearby trees rattle. The air smells cool and rainy. He walks through the hospital car park, out onto the street. He thinks of Juliet, of what his life will be like without her, of all the habits he will break. He will not go swimming any more. He will not sit with her in the evening, staring out the window. When he throws his die on to the backgammon board, no-one will say, 'Hold on, that was my turn!'

At the end of the street is a small garden, grown over with clematis. He sits on a bench and looks at the dark leaves of the vine, and cannot believe that in summer it will be covered in white flowers. He pulls out his phone and dials Hannah's number. When he hears her say 'Hello' he begins to speak, but soon realises it is an answerphone. He waits, clears his throat, speaks again. For the rest of the afternoon and evening, he stays at Juliet's side. He sits, holding her hand, staring at her, wishing she would wake. The nurse brings him a meal, which he leaves sitting on the table beside the bed.

He tells Juliet about the journeys they will take, in distant days, from Constance down the Rhine; from Maggiore to Como; down the Euphrates into the Adriatic, where they will dive to Atlantis and swim among its marble palaces and courtyards. As the night passes, he grows more and more tired. He leans his head against the bed and allows his eyelids to float down over his eyes, but he tries not to sleep, because he could not bear to miss her waking. He holds her skin-and-bone hand between his palms, as gently as he can. Sometimes, he raises his head far enough to touch his lips to the tips of her fingers.

Early the next morning, as the first, faint light comes into the room, he goes to the window and looks down on the street. It is busy now with people and cars. He looks closer, at the window ledge. A sparrow lands there and stares at him with its tiny, dark eye. He turns back to Juliet and continues his stories about the rivers of Europe, until he is too tired to go on. Finally, he falls asleep and dreams he is a boy of seven years old. His mother has dressed him in walk shorts and a pressed white shirt, and slicked his hair with a watered comb. She leads him by the hand out the front door, down the steps, along the path, to a waiting car. They climb into the back seat and the car pulls out into the street.

Soon it pulls over and he climbs out. He joins a crowd of children on the footpath. The children are excited. Some are nervous. They push towards a large door which opens in the side of a great, tall building. Most of the children are bigger than him. Some push and bustle. When they get inside, they follow a wide hallway and turn a corner into a large room. The walls are made of glass, and behind the glass is pale blue water. The water is thick with fish. There are so many he cannot watch one for more than a second before it is obscured by clouds of others.

Swimming among the fish is a little girl, with pale blue eyes and blonde hair, garlanded with roses, down to her waist. She swims, with graceful, flickering limbs, and recites, in a voice that sounds like wind-chimes, 'Don't hide! Don't hide! It's not so bad on the other side.'

'I wouldn't know,' Benjamin answers from the depths of his sleep. 'I'm too old to go there.'

At that moment, he wakes abruptly and thinks he sees Juliet's lips moving. He leans closer, but all is still.

'Juliet?' he whispers.

The night is calm and silent. Moonlight creeps in to the room, making it faintly blue. He touches her forehead and draws his hand back quickly. It is cold.

2.

Hannah flies straight back from London.

'I've missed you,' he says, when he meets her at the airport.

She squeezes his hand as they walk towards the luggage conveyor.

Later, she sits in Juliet's chair, with her back to the swaying treetops of the park outside. She fires questions at him. How did it happen? Why did she not seem ill just a few days before, when Hannah had been there? He gives patient, careful answers, feeling he owes her something, though he doesn't know why.

The funeral is held in a small wooden chapel on a hillside. Many of their friends have already died and the congregation is sparse. He wishes Hannah had children to bring. Children soften a funeral; they lack comprehension of loss.

The service is brief. Benjamin speaks, bravely, from the heart. Hannah reads a poem. Juliet's friends file out to the raindrop sounds of Satie's Gymnopedie No. 1. Tea and biscuits are served in a hall attached to the chapel. Benjamin stays for what he feels is the minimum allowable time before slipping out the back and going for a walk.

Thin, cold drizzle falls along the promenade. It breaks the sea's surface with tiny spots. Everything is grey. Past the beach, the road narrows and there is a gap in the sea wall. He follows a set of steps down to rocks below. Sitting on the lowest step, he removes his shoes, dips his feet into the tide, and cries.

Later, he returns to the apartment, carrying a brass urn containing Juliet's ashes.

'Where shall we put you?' he says, as he walks from room to room. 'Where would you like?'

He decides on a shelf in the living room, between a pot plant and a photograph of Hannah.

'There,' he says. 'That'll do.'

He raises his hand to his mouth. 'I'll not be one of those doddering old men who talks to his wife's ashes.'

He has resolved, since his walk by the sea, that he will not grieve. He tells himself she would want it that way. Besides, he feels certain he will see her again, one day. He will be on the balcony, looking down into the park, and she will walk along the pathway under the line of trees or he will take a stroll on the promenade, past the café, and see her in the window.

For the next few days he can hardly keep himself awake. Each night he goes to bed before sundown. He tries to read but the letters jumble before his eyes, and he finds himself nodding off after a sentence or two. 'I don't feel like a book,' he calls to the urn. 'I just want to lie here and think.' Within seconds his eyes have closed, his mouth has fallen open, he is snoring.

In the mornings he is woken by his bladder. He rises at six, shuffles to the bathroom, empties himself and shuffles back to bed, feeling that he has exerted himself too much. He sleeps a little more, then rises for breakfast, but the effort of slicing grapefruit and pouring cornflakes into a bowl makes him weary, so he curls up on the sofa for another nap. It is as if he has been poisoned. If he holds his hands before his face he cannot stop them from shaking. After a few weeks, he feels his strength returning. He climbs out of bed more readily, shaves for the first time since the funeral, eats an enormous breakfast.

'What shall we do today?' he asks Juliet.

He sets about cleaning the apartment, picking up clothes, wiping benches, mopping the floors. He makes his bed, dusts, vacuums until the carpet frays.

He fills a plastic bag with old blankets, pillows, sheets and towels. He fills another with pots, pans, cups, glasses, knives and forks yellow with tarnish. In the bedroom, he fills a bag with shoes and another two with clothes—his old business shirts and suits; Juliet's dresses, slacks, blouses, shorts, shirts and undergarments. He throws out magazines and videos, papers, electrical gadgets, ornaments, books he doesn't care for.

When he has finished, he carries each bag out into the hallway, along with the television set, the hi-fi, two radios and a few chairs, piling them all high and precarious. He phones the city mission and leaves a message, asking them to collect everything.

When he walks back into the apartment he is struck by its spartan appearance. He has left himself the easy chair; the bed; a small bookshelf containing his and Juliet's favourite books; some note-paper; a pen and some envelopes; their photographs; a few clothes, including his wedding suit and Juliet's wedding dress; and enough in the kitchen to cook with. The next day, he takes out some note-paper and the pen, and in neat script writes his own address and the date.

He writes,

'Dear Hannah, It was so nice to see you and so sad. I have always missed you. Thank you for returning so soon and being here when we needed you. You are a fine person and have made Juliet and me very proud.

'Don't worry about rushing away so soon. I understand you are busy. Perhaps when I see you next we will have time to reminisce a little and be happy.

'All my love,

'Benjamin (Dad).'

He writes several more notes to friends, relatives, acquaintances who were at the funeral. When he has finished, he puts them outside the door with a note to the mission workers, asking that the letters be posted.

He goes back into the apartment and sits down in the easy chair, which now faces a blank wall. He gets up and turns the chair towards the window. It is mid-afternoon. Pearly clouds fill the sky. The treetops are still. A gull flies past and swoops towards the harbour. Benjamin closes his eyes. He wants to clear his mind of these images, to conjure some of his own. He begins with his last memory —light, flickering, perhaps invented—of Juliet's lips moving at the moment of her death, and continues, in reverse order, through her last days, reliving each moment at her bedside, each touch of his hand on hers, each kiss of her forehead, each half-seen movement of her eyelids.

His memories are cinema shots, carefully framed: the book she read in bed the night before her stroke; her hands smoothing down the bedcovers; the television screen earlier that evening; the left-over pasta on her plate; her laugh at something he had done. What was it? Poked out his tongue? Pulled a face?

'I will leave some details for now,' he calls to the urn. 'Fill them in later.'

He continues, from last memory to first, summoning their shared lives, their life. A life spent swimming.

In the Schwansee at night—two beautiful white birds, illuminated by the moon. At Niagara, watching from downstream as a young American lunatic plunges over the falls in a barrel. In the Black Sea, buoyed up by its dense salt texture. In Rome, content in a bathhouse, basking in steam. Crossing the Cook Strait and the English Channel. Plunging into mountain streams and following them, down falls and rapids, along sedate, slow, braided bends. Splashing in the shallows of beaches. Hannah's birth, in a blood-darkened pool in a hospital ward. Their exchange of rings and vows, beside a duckpond, during a cloudburst, to a drum-roll of drizzle-pattered lilies.

Their first meeting, during a midwinter race, in which swimmers swarmed, tangling arms and legs, chopping the sea into tiny, white pieces, making it seethe and boil. He glimpsed her, up ahead, a woman with slender, sapling limbs, gliding through the water without seeming to displace a drop, trailing a garland of blonde hair. He swore she would not beat him to shore.

3.

Months have passed. The light is duller now, the air a little more bitter. The young trees along the path have grown a little—their trunks have thickened; they stand tall and military against the breeze. Benjamin walks with uncertain steps, across the park, past the docks, along the promenade. It has been a long time since he has left the apartment—a time lived in the fog of memory, amid the sheetfolds of dreams. He is conscious of the air, filled with the smell of salt, sharp and cold on his face.

As he walks, his memories of walking return. Once again, he grows used to the swing of arms, the steady stride forward, the rise and fall of his ribcage. His limbs lose their rustiness, become stronger, more confident. Walking, he decides, is like riding a bike. He turns to one side or another, expecting to see Juliet. He opens his mouth, to make some comment, catches it on the point of his tongue. When he reaches the crescent-shaped beach, he looks out across the glassy sea.

'Into the world again, my love,' he says.

And waits, vainly, for an answer.

Each morning from then, he rises at six and walks through the park, past the dock, along the promenade until he reaches a place where steep, golden cliffs rise beside the road. There he stops at a little byway jutting from the path, and sits awhile, looking out to sea.

One morning, on his homeward walk, he notices a man about his own age, white-haired and thin, walking towards the pinnacle where the cliffs begin. The man, well-dressed in a dark suit, fights the breeze, his limbs moving jerkily—but his face shows no evidence of his struggle; it is proud and expressionless. As they pass, Benjamin nods curtly.

The next morning, when they see each other again, they stop, touch their hands to their foreheads in salute.

'Pleasant morning,' says the man.

'Pleasant, indeed!' says Benjamin, somewhat too loudly. He has not spoken for so long, except to Juliet, and he speaks softly to her because she can hear his thoughts.

'My name is Joseph,' says the man, extending a hand, which Benjamin takes and shakes smartly.

'Benjamin,' he says.

'I used to see you swimming,' says Joseph, a bright reflection in his eye. 'With your wife.'

Benjamin shudders.

'You used to swim out to the headland and disappear. I used to worry you would get lost out there, you wouldn't find your way back.'

They walk together along the promenade and stop at an old-fashioned konditorei where they eat sweet pastries, drink coffee, and compare notes on their lives—each, like boys, eager to outdo the other.

'I have visited thirty-six countries,' Benjamin announces. 'On six continents.'

He lists them alphabetically. To each Joseph says 'Check!'. Then he adds three more of his own —Algeria, Crete and Martinique. Benjamin sips the cream from his coffee.

'I have a daughter,' he says, 'a journalist, in London.'

'Two daughters,' says Joseph. 'Professor at Oxford. Cellist in the New York Philharmonic. And a son, biophysicist, second in charge of the Genome Project.'

'My wife was beautiful,' says Benjamin.

'Mine was kind-hearted.'

'I was married for fifty-three years,' says Benjamin, slapping the table. His face reddens, his eyes develop a hard glaze.

Joseph shifts his chair. In a quiet voice, barely a clearing of his throat, he says, 'Fifty four and six months.'

The next morning, Benjamin is already seated at a table in the window overlooking the bay when Joseph arrives with a small black case under his arm. He lays it down with great ceremony, flicks its brass latches, and turns it over to expose the sixty-four squares of a chessboard. It is an expensive board, its squares alternating between grey slate and white shell. Without saying a word, Joseph draws the pieces from a leather pouch, lays them in their rows—taking white for himself—and advances his king's pawn to the fourth rank. Benjamin matches, pushing his king's pawn forward. Joseph advances his queen's pawn one square, and Benjamin counters with a knight. Joseph shakes his head, shifts his tongue against the roof of his mouth.

'I was the captain of my school football team,' he says. 'I once scored a goal from the halfway line.'

'I was the goalkeeper,' says Benjamin. 'Scored six times with lobs from my own goal-mouth. I'll admit the advantage of wind on one.'

'You didn't,' says Joseph.

'I didn't,' Benjamin agrees. 'I tried. I should have. It's never too late.'

Joseph advances his queen's knight, giving double protection to the pawn. He nods, firmly, approving the move. Benjamin brings a pawn out one rank. He is building a defensive wall.

'I was a sergeant during the war,' he says. 'Led a rescue mission behind enemy lines at Tobruk. Someone made a film of it, turned us all into Americans, changed it all around.'

'I was a wing commander,' says Joseph. 'Victoria Cross. Shot down twenty-six of the enemy. Took some fire across the tail and had to put my plane down in a field in the north of France. Watched her go up in flames. On my way to Dunkirk I was shot in the chest. Kept going on my hands and knees, sleeping under hedges in daylight, crawling at night. Swam the Channel in the small hours, scaled the Cliffs of Dover in the morning, climbed right into the arms of my beloved, who'd had breakfast waiting since half past eight. Hot coffee tastes good after a swim.'

'What rot,' says Benjamin.

'Partly,' Joseph admits.

The game goes on until mid-afternoon, when Joseph's rook traps Benjamin's king behind a line of pawns. It is the lamest defeat in chess, but the game has been hard fought. Both men are satisfied.

'Tomorrow?' Joseph asks, as they shake hands firmly.

'Tomorrow,' says Benjamin, fiercely.

They meet each day and play from sunrise to sunset, through storms that shake the cafe's foundations and days of sunshine so bright the coffee boils in its cups. Their games are wars, in which Joseph is the aggressor, sending rooks and knights on daring raids, arraying queens and bishops in flamboyant pincer attacks. Benjamin builds walls of pawns, rooks and bishops three ranks deep. They hold for hours and days, like earth walls holding back sea.

As Benjamin and Joseph play, they argue— about life, love, religion and sport. Each lists his greatest wars, favourite songs, best footballers, worst disasters, most breathtaking views. Many times they raise their voices in shouts that border on song, and turn their heads to see other diners staring. Always, their arguments end in handshakes, smiles, agreements to disagree, sometimes embraces in which they pat each other awkwardly on the shoulders.

'Darwin is the greatest thinker,' says Joseph. 'He turned life upon its head.'

'Einstein,' says Benjamin, thumping the table. 'He made time slow down, which makes him the patron saint of lovers.'

'Of the misunderstood,' says Joseph.

Benjamin sips his coffee, which has grown cold, as he likes it. For once, they will agree.

On the afternoons when their games finish early, he goes to the library and studies the masters. He learns the openings of Spassky and Fischer, and the devastating mid-game of Karpov. He reads biographies of Tal and Korchnoi, and books of theory and tactics. He learns that each of the masters is different, each like a poet. Kasparov is brutal, Spassky lyrical, Fischer aglow with mad brilliance. As Benjamin studies, he feels he is learning about the world. To understand openings, he studies the dances of atoms and how they give rise to life; to comprehend mid-games, he learns about syncopation and scales, fugues and variations; and, to get to grips with the end-game, he studies the tactics of predation—how chimpanzees communicate as they trap a macaque, how lions trail gazelles, how spiders lay traps for flies...

With each game, he feels he is improving. His defence is tougher than ever, his walls of pawns and knights more impregnable. Yet, ultimately, they succumb. This is the one constant of his relationship with Joseph. No matter how violent the struggle; no matter how quick and flamboyant, nor how much a test of stamina; no matter how many pieces Benjamin has standing at the end of the game, and how few are at Joseph's disposal, Benjamin always, always loses.

'Chess is the greatest game of all,' declares Joseph, after one, particularly emphatic victory. A look of mischief crosses his face. 'It is vastly superior to backgammon, for example.'

Benjamin feels as if he has been struck. His friend is being reckless, trying to provoke.

'You don't mean that,' he says. 'I see through your little joke.'

'It is no joke,' says Joseph. 'I am very serious. Never more so. In every way, chess is superior. It elucidates status, power, human nature in all its vileness.'

'Backgammon requires more luck, and therefore is more like life.'

'Chess is more calculating.'

'Backgammon more vicious.'

'Chess requires more mental dexterity. It demands strategy, and the flexibility to break from it. It requires forethought, and a masterly grasp of an opponent's frailties.'

'Backgammon,' Benjamin says, grasping. 'Backgammon is more sociable.'

'You resign, then?'

'Never!'

'You owe me a slice of gateau.'

The next morning, as Benjamin fends one of Joseph's volleys, and their two cups of coffee grow cold side by side, the conversation turns to greatest loves.

'Napoleon and Josephine?' Joseph inquires.

'Perhaps.'

'Samson and Delilah?'

'Narcissus and himself?'

Benjamin moves his rook forward three ranks, putting Joseph's king in check, but also exposing his own.

'This is silly,' he says, leaning forward, looking Joseph in the eye. 'There is no greater love than Juliet's and mine.'

Joseph smiles. He moves his king one file to the right, protecting it behind a bishop.

'You really compare it to Romeo and Juliet?' he asks.

'Of course,' says Benjamin. 'In any case, ours was real. Romeo was just a story. In life, he never got near her. I saw to that. I had our balcony glassed in.'

'Well, my friend, could yours and mine win the silver medal?'

'Of course,' says Benjamin. 'Silver is still good. You can take away a world record, but never a medal.'

Joseph moves his queen from its position, protecting the king, seven squares on the diagonal. He stops it two squares from Benjamin's king. Checkmate. Benjamin throws his hands in the air.

'You're too good for me,' he says. 'I'll never win.'

'Nonsense,' says Joseph. 'You don't want to win. You play for the draw. Perhaps to make the game last longer.'

Benjamin shrugs.

'I suppose you're right,' he says.

'Winning means something to me,' Joseph continues. 'You just like the company.'

Outside the café, before they part, they shake hands.

'I like you,' says Benjamin. He smiles, turns quickly, and begins to walk along the promenade towards his home. The next morning, Benjamin skips his morning walk and does not appear in the café. He lies on the sofa in his living room, staring at the ceiling, a mug of coffee beside him. He spends the day trying to revive his memories. He thinks of the mermaid he dreamed of the night Juliet died; her fatal slip on the bedroom floor; the backgammon board set up for play as they sat together the previous night. He brings back anniversaries and birthdays, the storm of their wedding—but he can't remember what city they were in or who the guests were, and he can't remember whether he was able to remember the last time he tried. His memories have faded. Where once they were clear and bright, now he sees them through gauze.

'Has it come to this, my love?' he asks the urn. 'Has it been so long?'

He sits in silence, with his head in his hands, clearing his mind, but when he tries again it is worse. He can see nothing but whiteness, like a television screen showing static.

The next morning, he returns to the café and plays with fury. He repels each attack with fire, and makes his own guerrilla forays into Joseph's end of the board—but Joseph parries each advance and builds a wall about his king, three rows deep in all directions, closing off the diagonals, the zigzag movements of knights, the straightforward lines of rooks. It is a mined maze.

Their game lasts all day. The noon sun is so bright it makes the pieces too hot to handle— Joseph fetches two dishcloths from the kitchen to hold them with—and the evening sun turns everything to amber, making it difficult for Benjamin and Joseph to tell their pieces apart. By sundown both are exhausted. Joseph's face is hollow and gaunt. Benjamin can hardly keep his eyes open. Both would gladly shake hands and agree to a draw but neither can open his dry lips to make the suggestion. It is Joseph's turn and he has taken a long time. Once in a while his eyes slip shut and breath whistles from his nostrils. Finally, he lifts a pawn in front of his king and moves it one place forward.

'But,' says Benjamin, eyeing the clear diagonal now open before Joseph's king. With three movements, of knight and queen, it will be over. 'Are you sure?'

Joseph's hand hovers over the board, then falls back to his lap.

'Is it a trick?' Benjamin asks.

'Shh,' Joseph interrupts. He opens his mouth as if to speak, then closes it again and turns to look out the window. 'If you had never met her,' he says, 'would you have missed her? Could you have loved someone else or would you have spent your life waiting for Juliet?'

Benjamin moves his knight forward, pinning his friend's queen and rook, exploiting the opening his friend has made.

'I would have missed her,' he says. 'I would have waited.'

Joseph moves his queen several squares away, to safety. Benjamin advances his knight to take the rook.

'How about you,' he says. 'Could you have loved anyone else?'

Joseph picks up his king and weighs it in his palm. Something in his expression—the way he narrows his eyes, the way he forms his words slowly and precisely—seems very familiar to Benjamin.

'Yes,' Joseph says, 'I never did, but if I found myself alone I could have.'

He lays the king gently on its side and pushes his stool away from the table.

'What? Are you conceding?'

Joseph reaches across the table and takes Benjamin's hand. For a few moments he holds it gently.

'I know all I need to,' he says.

With a sweep of his arm he rolls the chess pieces into their case and clips it shut. Then he stands sharply and walks to the door.

'Wait!' Benjamin calls, but by the time he has risen from his chair and got to the door his friend has disappeared into the black night.

4.

Very early, before first light, before the air has lost its chill, Benjamin rises from the bed he shared with Juliet for so long. He showers, pats a little cologne on his cheeks, and dresses in his wedding suit. From his apartment it is a short walk across the park where trees with solid trunks stand tall against the breeze, past the docks where the cruise liners berth.

'Here we are, my love,' he says, when he is standing alongside their beach. 'Another morning swim.'

He stoops and places the urn in the sand, pushing it in to make sure it doesn't tip. He removes his tie first, rolling it and putting it in his jacket pocket. He has shrunk in his later years and the jacket flaps like a flag. He slips it off and lies it on the sand beside the urn. His unbuttoned shirt reveals a sunken chest, with the soft flesh over his heart and ribs showing plainly below. He folds the shirt and lays it on the jacket, then removes his shoes and socks, placing them beside the growing pile of clothes. When he loosens the belt, his trousers slide down of their own accord.

He stands tall in his swimming trunks, a man of a proud age, who has lived a good life, surveying the curve of the harbour, the buildings opposite, the sea's white breakers.

'After all this time,' he says, stooping and lifting the urn to his side, 'I don't know what to say. I'm not a man for ceremonies, I don't have a speech. I loved you, that's all. I still love you. I always will.'

The water is ice-cool, licking at his shins, slicking down white hairs. As he walks in deeper, it laps his knees, his thighs. He shudders when it reaches his scrotum. In the past he might have splashed it to quicken the pain, but now thinks only of the urn. When the water is waist-deep he stops.

'It's time,' he whispers, raising the urn to his face and kissing it, then lowering it to sea level and twisting its lid. A slick of blue-grey dust spreads across the water, like a storm cloud in an otherwise clear sky. Soon it is caught by the tide and breaks up. A single tear rolls down Benjamin's cheek. Another follows. Soon tears are pouring from his eyes, spreading over his cheeks, running into the corners of his mouth. Through his tears he sees, far off across the bay, a patch of red on the ocean's surface. At first it seems like a reflection of lights from some ship or building, but soon another patch forms. Before long, it seems that half of the harbour is covered in its glow. He looks skyward, at scudding clouds, rain-heavy and pink.

'My love,' he says, closing his eyes.

When he opens them again the whole ocean is red. He runs his hand through it and lifts to his face a bright red petal. The bay is filled with roses. Everywhere he looks they bloom, rising and falling with the tide. The air is filled with their scent. He plunges into the pink-tinged water and swims beyond the curve of beach, along the line of scarlet rocks, into the rose-covered harbour depths. When he is near the island he turns and looks back at the hills, the cliff-nestled houses whose windows reflect pink, the high-rises, the tops of the trees in the park beside his building.

Clouds speed overhead, blown by a vicious wind. A single raindrop lands on his face. He reaches up a hand and wipes it away, and for the briefest, flickering moment, as if red lenses have dropped from his eyes, the sea is blue-black, the sky grey, the hills green, and the windows of houses reflect white light. Waves, lapping on the metal-grey beach, whisper 'so far, so far', and pain ices through his heart, for in this lucid moment he sees himself for what he is: an old man who has stripped himself nearly naked and plunged into the sea, and swum so far out he will not have the strength to go back, because he has been fooled by love.

Ice

Jan saw the advertisement in the morning newspaper. She was sitting at the table in her two-room flat. Pale grey light came through the window and settled across the page. 'The Hotel Artemis,' the ad said, in heavy, gothic lettering. There was a picture of it, a black-and-white sketch —three storeys tall with balconies and turrets, and a backdrop of snow-covered mountains. 'One night with us and you will never want to go home.' She tore it out, folded it carefully, and put it in her pocket. She liked to read the travel page because she had never travelled and dreamed of doing so. When she read to Francis of far-off places —great cities, mountains, lakes, deserts—they twisted in her telling until it was no longer clear what was real and what she had imagined.

'Francis,' she called sleepily. 'It's time to get up.'

He stirred slowly in his bed in the corner of the room, rubbed his eyes, yawned, kicked off his bed-covers.

'Morning, my love,' she said.

'Morning, Mum,' he replied.

After they had eaten breakfast, and Francis had washed and dressed, Jan took his hand and led him down the stairs and out into the dusty heat of morning. When they reached his school, she bent and kissed him and watched as he ran into the playground and was lost amid a bright blur of children. Throughout the day at work, she dreamed she was at the hotel, sitting in a cosy room with a fire going, looking out the window at wind-blown snow. After work, as she walked back to the school, she imagined her feet scrunching snow on the pavement. She reached the school at five minutes to three and waited by a little stream than ran through its grounds. A willow tree grew on its banks, and its dry leaves hung down into the trickle of water. Francis came running towards her.

'Hello!' he yelped, wrapping his arms around her and burying his face in her lap.

On their way home they stopped at O'Malley's. As Jan sipped her tea and Francis licked an ice cream, she took the advertisement from her pocket and showed it to him. Together, they studied the turrets and balconies, which seemed, in the soft light of the café, to rise from the page and shimmer before them.

'Would you like to go to this place?' Jan asked. 'Would you like to go on holiday?'

'Maybe,' said Francis. 'But, how cold is ice?'

Jan took his ice cream and bit into it, holding the small cold pearl of sweetness on her tongue. As she handed the ice cream back she dabbed it against his cheek.

'As cold as that,' she said.

36

Francis whooped: 'That's cold!' Other customers turned and looked at him. Mrs O'Malley waddled over and peered at the picture, then shrugged and waddled back to the till. Francis crunched into the cone and chewed noisily.

The next morning, Jan sent off an email and transferred the payment. For the next few weeks she packed and unpacked bags, each time trying to fit more into less. She used the last of her savings to buy Francis a new coat of blue oilskin with a thick wool lining. She made him model it for her. He tried the coat on, zipping and unzipping it, and spinning and spinning until he fell over dizzy. Jan bit her lip as she watched; no-one could love anyone as she loved him.

The day they set out was hot and clear. A northerly blew across rooftops, swaying trees and whipping up leaves. The river sparkled, a bright glare reflected from the streets. As the last suburban house disappeared behind them and the flat yellow expanse of plains opened up, Jan asked, 'Are you ready?' and Francis did a thumbs-up. For two hours the road went in a straight line. The plains spread out before them, golden and dry, bent under layers of silver light.

Before long Francis curled his legs up in his seat and leaned his head against the door and fell asleep. Jan drove in a kind of trance, listening to the sound of his breath. After a while, the light outside greyed and the road began to climb into foothills. Rain fell, lightly at first, then in heavy sheets. Jan could just see the car's bonnet, and beyond, lit up by the headlamps, the pale edges of the road. Francis woke up and began to chatter to himself.

'It's a whale out there,' he said. 'Look at the whale!' In a different voice, high-pitched, he argued: 'No! It's a shark!' Jan imagined the grey mass of rain circling the car *was* a shark. She saw its fin rising and its sharp teeth glinting in the headlights. She pressed the accelerator and allowed the car to swerve a little.

'Ga-dunk!' said Francis.

'Did I get it?' she asked. 'Did I get ten points?'

'You got twenty,' he said. 'It was B-I-G!'

The road narrowed as they climbed into the mountains, and snowdrifts grew in steep banks on either side until Jan felt she was driving in a tunnel. She slowed the car to a crawl, keeping it in second gear. Francis stared out the window silently. He was dressed in his new coat, and looked warm and peaceful and serious.

'What's on your mind?' she asked.

He shrugged.

'What can you see?'

She pulled the car slowly around a bend. Up ahead they could see the tips of pine trees rising from a gully, and snow-covered hills, and cold blue mountain peaks. The road zigzagged up the side of one of the hills—a snaking grey line in a vista of white.

'Snow,' Francis said. 'Snow! Snow! Snow! Snow! Snow!'

'And?'

'Ice!'

'You don't mean ice spy?'

He giggled. 'I spy,' he said, 'with my little eye, something beginning with M.'

'Mountain?' she said.

'No.'

'Mummy?'

'No, silly,' he said. 'It's *me*!'

As they rounded another bend they saw the hotel. Jan stopped the car in front and looked at the building, veiled in mist, blending in to the mountainside. Its white walls could have been just another snow-covered ridge, its round turret a minor peak.

With a suitcase in each hand, Jan climbed the steps to the entrance. The door was almost twice her height, made of panelled wood. Jan pushed and it swung open with a faint creak, revealing the foyer: a tall, narrow cavern in which everything was white. The walls, on which appeared images of mountains and hills, seemed to glow as if they had been carved from blocks of ice. The ceiling, which seemed impossibly high, was glass and allowed a view of pale sky. The floor was of marble, overlayed with clear crystal tiles, and ahead, at the end of the long, narrow room, almost lost in shadows, a marble staircase rose so high Jan could not see its top.

As she was looking around she heard a voice call: 'Hello.' She looked up and saw a woman on the stairs. 'I'm Mrs Stiller,' the woman called. 'Your host.' Mrs Stiller was very tall and thin, dressed from head to toe in a long, flowing white gown, which concealed her feet and made it appear as if she was gliding. As she came closer, Jan saw that her hair, too, was long and white, reaching almost down to her waist, and her skin was so pale it was almost translucent. Her face was narrow with a thin, hooked nose, her lips bloodless, her eyes piercing, with irises and pupils that merged because both were as black as obsidian. 'I'm very pleased to see you,' she said, extending a thin, bony hand. Jan was surprised by the tightness of her grip, and the thin black lattice of veins on her wrist. Mrs Stiller smiled, but even her smile was thin. 'Come with me,' she said.

They followed her across the foyer, up the staircase and across the landing. At the end of a dimly lit corridor, they came to a door. Mrs Stiller turned its handle and it swung open, revealing their room, vast and bright. At its centre was a four-poster bed covered in heavy white brocade, and beside that was another bed—smaller, otherwise identical. In one corner was a writing table and a chair. At the end of the room was a set of windows and a pair of glass doors opening onto a balcony from which they saw a grand view of a mountainside. As Jan looked around, Mrs Stiller followed, pointing out small details—a jug of ice water on a table between the beds; a crystal chandelier; a shelf with tiny white porcelain sculptures—a deer, a dog, a swan, all sleeping.

'They look so real,' Jan said.

Mrs Stiller blushed, her pale skin showing a delicate dusting of scarlet. She said it was quiet at the hotel when there were no guests and she liked to make things.

'Did *you* make them?' Jan exclaimed. 'You're very clever!'

Mrs Stiller laughed.

'Well,' she said. 'I'll leave you two alone now. Dinner will be ready in an hour. The dining room is at the other end of the corridor, past the stairs.'

'Thank you,' said Jan. 'Thank you so much.'

When Mrs Stiller had gone, Jan kept looking around the room. Near the writing table was a shelf full of books, all bound in white leather covers with silver lettering: *The Silver Chair*; *The Snow Queen*; *The White Witch*. Near the shelf was a trolley with a kettle and several tins containing teas Jan had never heard of—persimmon, nettle, oleander and broom. In the bathroom were tiny glass bottles containing shampoos and perfumes and lotions. She unscrewed their lids and sniffed them. One smelled of mint and made her feel cool and alert; another smelled of jasmine and made her feel mildly, sweetly drunk. She found the wardrobes already full of clothes—in one hung long gowns, trousers, jackets and blouses, and in the other hung little suits, bow-ties, shorts, shirts, shoes and socks. When Jan tried the bed it seemed to give way beneath her as if she was falling through clouds. Down, down she went, feeling confused and mildly dizzy, but at the last moment it caught her and gathered her in its downy softness.

'Oh my God,' she exclaimed. 'This is so wonderful.'

On the wall beside the bed was a painting that, at first glance, seemed to be merely textured paint —but when Jan caught it at an angle she saw, very faintly, like a shadow, a woman's face, smooth and narrow, with long tousled hair, very like her own. As she looked closer she saw that the woman was standing beside a stream, and beside her was a little boy who held her hand.

Jan appeared at dinner dressed in a long, flowing white gown, with a rose in her hair, and Francis wore a white suit with a crisp shirt and bow tie. A white kerchief, folded in the shape of mountain peaks, was in his pocket. The dining room was so grand it left Jan breathless. It was enormous, with a table so large it could seat fifty, and a huge fireplace in which a flames flickered thinly.

'Don't you two look fabulous?' Mrs Stiller said as she showed them to their seats. 'I could eat you all up.'

At the end of the table away from the fire, three places were set up with silver cutlery and crystal glasses. Jan sat on one side and Francis on the other, leaving a place at the top for Mrs Stiller, who disappeared through a door and reappeared a moment later, pushing a trolley containing several silver dishes. 'I hope we all like mountain trout,' she said. She lifted the lid from the largest of the dishes and revealed the fish, cooked whole on a small hill of rock salt. Its skin was black but when she sliced it open its flesh was the softest creamy white. With the fish she served leeks in a roux sauce and tiny boiled potatoes. Jan found each bite delicious, though it quickly dissolved on her tongue and when she swallowed she felt as if she was ingesting air. As they ate, Jan asked if there were any other guests. Mrs Stiller smiled. She reached both hands across the table, taking Francis's hand in one and Jan's in the other.

'No,' she said. 'Just you.'

After dinner, as Jan bathed Francis in water scented with spearmint, he asked her why Mrs Stiller's hand had been so cold, and she explained that sometimes older people had cold hands and feet because of their circulation. After the bath she dressed him in the pure white silk pyjamas she had found under his pillow, and she tucked him into her own bed. He lay, quite still, with his eyes wide open, staring at the ceiling. Jan cuddled up close to him. She kissed his forehead and stroked his hair, and after a while he started to grow sleepy, his eyes closed, his breathing grew slow and steady.

In the morning they were woken by a thin stream of sunlight filtering through the glass doors.

Jan pulled on a dressing gown and went out on to the balcony to look at the mountainside. Francis appeared at her side and tugged on her gown.

'Can we go out, Mum? Can we have a look?'

At breakfast he was silent and fidgety, but once they were back in their room, dressing in their coats and gloves and boots and woollen hats, he cheered up. Jan took him by the hand and led him along the corridor, down the staircase and out through glass doors to a courtyard laid with crystal tiles. Francis bent his knees and skidded, dragging Jan with him. Beyond the courtyard was a narrow path which led a few steps on to the mountainside before it was lost under a dense carpet of snow. Jan walked up the mountain, each footstep sinking in deep. Francis ran on ahead, until he was just a faint grey smudge in the distance.

His voice echoed back to her.

'I am a lion,' he yelled. 'Graaaa-urrrr.'

He came running towards her, then stopped, bent down, and arched his body. Something thumped into her leg and she looked down and saw, on her boot, the already disintegrating remains of a snowball.

I am a *big* lion,' he yelled.

She trudged towards him, catching up as he was making another snowball.

'Are you a snow lion?' she asked, laughing.

He stopped making the snowball while he thought. Then he came up close to her. She knelt in the snow and hugged him.

'I *am* a snow lion,' he whispered.

He broke away and went back to making the snowball.

'What else lives in the snow?' Jan asked.

He finished making the snowball and threw it. It landed with a soft *plump*. He ran after it with arms out wide.

'Polar bear!' he yelled. 'Graaaaa-uuuur!'

'What else?' she asked.

'Elephant.'

'Elephant?'

'Leopard,' he said.

'Snow leopard.'

'Yes.'

They walked on up the hillside. Gradually Jan became used to the snow. She took small, light steps, not allowing her feet to linger long enough to sink in. When she reached the crest she saw a vast plateau rising up to a ridge, and beyond that a line of spiky, snow-capped mountains, like a row of dogs' teeth. Francis plunged on to the plateau and began to run.

'This is fun!' he yelled. 'So, so fun!' He ran in zigzags, then doubled back and turned the Z shape he had made into a blocky figure of eight. 'Come on,' he yelled.

Jan stepped tentatively off the ridge, lost her footing and rolled in the snow.

'Yay-ay-ay,' Francis yelled. He dropped to his knees and together they rolled down the gentle slope—Francis first, Jan going faster and faster as she tried to catch up. When she came within reach she scrabbled at his coat.

'Missed me!' he sang. 'Missme missme missme.'

But while he sung he forgot to roll, so when she rolled over again she caught him.

'Gotcha!' she cried. Francis laughed. He got to his feet and ran. Jan sat in the snow and watched.

'I am a flying kangaroo,' he said. 'I am a kangaroo with skis!'

The first snowflakes were soft, star-shaped, floating slowly from a blue sky, but soon the sky became a dense, greyish white and the flakes came more heavily. Before long, Jan couldn't see further than the white tips of her gloves. She wished she had dressed Francis in his blue coat, not the white one left by Mrs Stiller.

'Francis?' she called.

She ran towards where she had last seen him— a little up the hill, a little to her left. Her feet sank deep into the snow and she had to stop and lift them out. She continued calling, calling, but he gave no answer. With the storm a wind had risen, filling the plateau with its faint, eerie whistle. She thought she glimpsed Francis through a break in the snowfall and ran, tripping, towards him, but it was just a black rock. A moment later, she again thought she saw him, out of the corner of her eye, but it was a shaft of pale sunlight breaking through the clouds behind her.

After some time, she came to a ridge where the hills plunged away steeply into a valley. The storm had eased and she could see the snow-covered valley floor and beyond to cliffs of black rock. She approached the ridge slowly and called again. Francis answered, in a light voice. 'I'm down here.'

She peered over and saw him, halfway down a steep, zigzag path which was cut into the cliff.

'Are you all right?' she called.

He stopped, looked up towards her, raised his arm in a big wave.

'Hurry up!' he called.

The path was narrow, lined with snow. Jan took small, careful steps, not daring to look up from her feet. When she reached the bottom, Francis was standing there, legs astride, hands on hips.

'You're slow!' he said.

She knelt and kissed him.

'I was scared,' she said. 'I couldn't see you.'

Francis looked at her.

'You shouldn't worry,' he said.

The valley floor was covered in long, thin snowdrifts, interrupted here and there by outcrops of rock. A thin, shallow stream flowed down one edge, near the cliffs.

Francis started walking up the valley, taking big strides. Jan looked at the sky and could see, directly overhead, shielded behind grey clouds, the broad outline of the sun. She jogged a few steps, catching up with Francis, and put her arm over his shoulder. They walked on until they reached the stream. Its water was smooth and clear as glass, and it flowed over stones that had been polished into flat discs and were as pale as the snow itself.

As they walked upstream the flat stony land of the valley began to give way to tall ragged rock spires. The stream flowed through narrow crevices and openings which Jan and Francis clambered through. 'Shhh,' Jan whispered. 'Can you hear it?' Not far off, hidden behind a wall of rocks, was the sound of a waterfall.

'This way,' Francis said, running through a narrow gap between two of the spires. Jan squeezed through behind him and found herself in a circular grotto. Before her, the waterfall streamed down a tall, black cliff, filling the air with mist.

Jan glanced around the walls of the grotto and counted seven statues made of ice.

She approached the first, a woman about her own age, dressed in a long coat and heavy boots, but taller, more slender. The woman's eyes were clear, her features perfect—a long, slim nose, flowing hair, thin lips formed into a serene smile. Jan ran her hands over the woman's face, feeling her skin. It did not stick like ice, but was smooth, liquid, glinting like quicksilver. Jan felt as if something of the woman's serenity, her perfect calmness, flowed through her fingertips.

The next statue was of a girl, who knelt in the snow, with her hands clasped together before her. Her face, like the woman's, was slender and perfect —her nose small, her hair long, her ears like tiny buttons—but her eyes were pixie-ish, and her lips curved into a mischievous grin.

The next was a man, lying in the snow, sleeping. He was strongly-built, with wavy hair down to his shoulders, a weathered face, and almond-shaped eyes. The next two were younger men, one tall, one short, and the next a dog—a labrador—which had rolled on to its back. The last was a man, much older than Jan, tall and strong, but stooped. One of his hands was outstretched, and his face— though thickly bearded—was frozen in an expression of pure anguish. His mouth was open, his eyes wide and glassy, his brow ridged. Jan touched his face but drew back quickly. The ice of his skin felt sharp, almost as if a mild electric current ran through it.

Francis touched her sleeve.

'Mum,' he said. 'Mum. Are these real people? They look like real people who are frozen.'

Jan shrugged.

'Mrs Stiller is very clever,' she said.

The sun, by then, was starting to dip behind the mountain. 'Come on,' said Jan. 'It's time to go.'

It was only after they had walked back down the valley, climbed the zigzag track and crossed the plateau that Jan realised how far they had come. From the ridge of the plateau she looked down on the hotel, but it was only a tiny speck far across the hillside, like a jewel lying in the snow.

They reached the hotel just before nightfall, and went straight to the dining room, where Mrs Stiller was waiting. She seated Jan and Francis opposite each other, and took her own place at the head of the table.

'We went exploring,' Francis said.

Mrs Stiller served up—a pale risotto, butter beans, boiled potatoes.

'Yes,' Jan laughed. 'I think we went a bit far.'

'Oh?' said Mrs Stiller. 'Where did you go?'

Jan described the walk she and Francis had taken—up the hillside, across the plateau, down into the ravine. She described the blizzard they had been through and the burnt orange sunset on the hill of fresh snow.

'We saw the ice people,' said Francis. 'They were cool. They were like they were alive.'

Mrs Stiller frowned. Jan wondered if she was nervous with new guests—as she herself might be if she had grown used to solitude.

'They were very good,' Jan said.

'One tries to keep busy,' Mrs Stiller replied.

Jan asked if she ever exhibited them.

'No. They're not for show.'

'Ferry gooth!' said Francis, his mouth full of beans. 'Ferry gooth intheeth!'

'Manners,' said Jan, winking at him.

Mrs Stiller smiled.

'I was surprised you wanted to come here,' she said. 'I get so few guests now. People don't want all this—', she motioned over the empty plates, '—this peace and quiet. They don't want out-of-the-way.'

For the first time, Jan realised just how old Mrs Stiller was. Her face seemed to have very little flesh —it was just a skull with skin stretched over it— and the skin itself was covered in a network of tiny wrinkles, as if spiders had spent years spinning layer upon layer of webs around her. The strange, charcoal irises of her eyes flickered, reflecting the firelight, and her forehead and nose cast long, wisping shadows.

Suddenly, Francis leapt from his chair and fled the room. Jan excused herself and followed, out into the corridor, across the landing.

'Darling?' she called. 'Francis?'

The bedroom door was open. Francis was lying on her bed, his face in the pillow.

'What's wrong?' she asked. 'What happened?'

Francis took a heavy breath and let it out with a sob. Jan lay beside him, holding him tight, as if her embrace was the only thing keeping him alive. After a while his breathing grew softer and more regular. He looked up at her, wide-eyed.

'Her face,' he said. 'It was like she was dead.'

She stroked his hair.

'It's okay,' she whispered. 'It's okay, it's okay, it's okay.'

His breathing stilled.

'It's okay?'

'Yes.'

He smiled. She saw the last of his tears run into the corners of his mouth.

'Once upon a time,' she said, 'in a land not far from here.'

His eyes widened.

'There was a little boy, whose name was Francis.'

A smile grew on his face.

'It's a good name,' he said.

'Who lived with his mother in a little flat, in a great big town.'

'Okay.'

Francis's mother loved him very much. So much she sometimes thought she would burst open like a balloon and her love would rush out and fill the air. She was very happy with her life, and the only thing that frightened her was that Francis would one day go off and leave her alone, because that's what people do.

One winter, the city they lived in became very cold. Every night, as the wind blew and icy rain fell, Francis's mother dressed him up very warm and tucked him into a warm bed. She brought him a drink of warm cocoa, and she told him a story, because Francis loved stories. She told him about all the places in the world, places where the ocean was so clear you could breathe its water and where the ice was so warm you could swim in it. Francis listened to her stories and went to sleep happy, and had the best dreams he could imagine.

But one night it was colder than ever and after his mother had gone to bed, Francis lay awake and looked out the window. Its pane was covered in frost, lit up by the street lamp outside. His breath came out in a great plume, his hands were so cold he had to put them under the covers, and his ears burned. While he was lying awake, looking out the window, snow began to fall. The flakes were very light. Some were shaped like stars, others like tiny leaves. After a while the snow became heavier, and the flakes fell harder. He heard them against his windowpane and landing on the ground below. One of the biggest snowflakes struck the window and landed on the ledge outside. It was the biggest snowflake he had ever seen, and when it landed, it began to grow even bigger. It grew and grew until it took up the whole window, and then it shattered and a woman stepped out. She was very tall and thin, with long, white hair, and she was dressed in a long gown of white fur. Her eyes were like little stars, and her mouth a narrow line of bluish-white. Her skin was made entirely of ice.

'Francis,' she said, in a voice that sounded like the wind, 'Will you come with me? Will you come and see the far corners of the earth?'

Francis was very excited. He had always wanted to see the far corners of the earth, so he leapt from his bed and opened the window. The air was so cold it was like steam. It poured over the window-ledge and swirled around the room, and when Francis could see nothing but this white air, the woman stepped forward. Francis, in his pyjamas and bare feet, shivered.

'Where will you take me?' he whispered.

'To the very ends of the earth,' said the woman.

From her belt she drew a knife with a silver handle and a blade of glinting ice. She waved it and said some magic words and Francis suddenly didn't feel cold any more. He felt quite warm. His hands were like toast and his feet felt like they did when he sat with them close to the heater. He looked up at the ice woman and saw that she was quite beautiful. Her face was long and slender, with a slim nose and a small, round chin. Her eyes shone. She took a step towards him and kissed him on the forehead, which made him feel very happy and safe. Then she enveloped him in her cloak, which, he saw now, was made from the feathers of some white bird—an albatross perhaps.

'Shall we count to three?' said the woman. Francis counted, and when he reached 'three' the woman bent her knees and sprung forward, carrying him under her arm. They flew out the window, across the street, over the snow-covered park, over the houses and buildings of the suburbs, over the mountains, and far away. As they flew, Francis *could see the spires of churches and the tops of trees. He could see people who looked like tiny dolls, and cars and trucks like toys. Then they flew higher and higher until he could see nothing but clouds below, and nothing above but daytime stars.*

After a while they started to descend. They went through the clouds and Francis saw a vast blue ocean and a continent made entirely of ice. He could see penguins marching across it, and a whale just offshore. Down they went, diving through the chill air. They flew along a valley, up over a mountain, down past cliffs and rocky crags, until they came to a cave.

'This is my home,' the woman told Francis. Its walls were carved out of ice, its ceiling was ice. Its floor was a frozen lake. The whole place was lit up by the southern lights...

Francis was asleep. Jan watched his eyes move under his eyelids, and his little chest rise and fall. His breathing was soft. Quietly, she reached over to the wall and switched off the lamp. Moonlight came into the room, making its pale walls shimmer. Jan fell asleep and dreamed that she was searching the far corners of the earth, and when she found the ice cave she gathered Francis up in her arms and flew with him back to the city. On the way she made a wish, and the cave melted into the ocean.

In the morning, Jan had Mrs Stiller leave their breakfast outside the door. When Francis woke he turned over in the bed and smiled.

'Are you okay this morning?' Jan asked.

Francis laughed.

'I'm good.' He looked at her quizzically. 'Aren't I?'

Outside the glass doors she could see snow falling heavily. It made a pattering sound against the pane, like the sound of something trying to get in. The sky was dull and white.

'Look,' said Jan. 'It's snowing hard.'

'It's snowing like a rocket,' said Francis. 'It's snowing like pea soup.'

She gathered him in her arms and held him.

'Shall we look at the snow?' she said.

They climbed out of bed and went to the window. The hillside was lost behind a curtain of snow, and the balcony outside was thickly covered. Jan could hear the wind blowing.

'I like snow,' said Francis. 'It's my favourite.'

His face was a full moon.

'Can we go out?' he said. 'Can we play in the snow?'

Jan shook her head.

'Not now,' she said. 'If it stops, maybe. You'll catch a cold.'

Francis looked disappointed.

'We could look around the hotel instead,' she said. 'We could go exploring.'

'Exploring,' said Francis. He skipped across the room. 'Exploring like an explorer does.'

She dressed him in a pair of white trousers, with a shirt and pullover and pale leather shoes, and she put on a white pants-suit and a white jacket. Moments later two heads leaned out of their doorway, checking Mrs Stiller wasn't in the corridor.

'Shhh,' said Francis. 'Go on tiptoes.'

So they tiptoed along the corridor and they tiptoed down the marble stairs and, though its crystal floor was slippery to walk on, they tiptoed across the foyer. The first door they came to was ajar. Jan pushed and it swung open with a loud creak.

'Shush,' said Francis, his finger to his lips.

The room was so large they could barely see its far wall, and so high the ceiling was lost in shadows. Along each wall, in each corner, in every inch of available space, were marble statues. Like the statues in the hills, all were of people; many of them children. Their features were perfect—eyes bright, mouths slightly open as if they were taking in breath. Jan walked from one to another, touching them, feeling their sharp coldness on her fingertips.

'Look,' said Francis.

Jan turned and saw two large blocks of ice, untouched.

'Are these going to be new ones?' he asked.

Jan said nothing. She looked for the door.

'How do we get out of here?' she asked. 'Please,' she said. 'I want to leave.'

She heard a creak and saw a door opening. She moved towards it, following the sound of Francis's footsteps.

'Francis?'

She squinted and rubbed her eyes. When she took her hands away, she saw that she was in the foyer. Francis took her hand.

'Mummy,' he said. 'I'm tired.'

He led her across the crystal floor, up the marble stairs, along the corridor, into their room. He lay down on his bed, Jan on hers. Just before she went to sleep she glanced over at him. His skin was pale, his eyes dull and dark. She decided she didn't like the mountains, she didn't like ice, she didn't like Mrs Stiller. When they woke from their sleep she would pack their bags and take Francis home.

'Sleep well, sweets,' she said.

Soon afterwards, she awoke and saw Francis standing by the window, his face pressed to the pane. She rolled over, buried her face in the pillow and went back to sleep. When she woke again the sun was low in the sky. Its pale light filled the room with soft shadows. She called out to Francis but there was no answer. She climbed out of bed and went to the window and looked out. Snow was still falling heavily. She checked under the beds, behind the curtains, in the bathroom.

'Francis?' she called.

She hurried along the corridor and checked the dining room. Its white fire burned in the grate but the room was empty. She went down the staircase, across the foyer, into the statue room. Mrs Stiller was there, carving one of the fresh blocks of marble. She looked up when Jan came in.

'Have you seen Francis?' Jan asked.

Mrs Stiller didn't answer.

'He's missing,' said Jan.

Mrs Stiller shrugged and continued to work on the block of marble. Jan moved closer and saw her own image emerging from its blankness. 'What are you doing?' she shrieked, grabbing hold of Mrs Stiller's arm. Mrs Stiller took a step to the side and slipped from Jan's grasp.

'Where is he?' Jan cried.

Mrs Stiller took her hand. 'On the mountain,' she said. 'He likes it there.'

Jan raced out into the foyer, slipping on the crystal tiles. Snow had piled against the doors and they stuck hard. When she struck them with her open hand they sprung open. She ran through the courtyard, on to the mountainside. Far off in the distance, the ridge and the sky blurred together. Everything was grey.

'Francis,' she called. An icy wind howled across the plateau.

'Francis!'

When she reached the ridge she stopped and rested. The valley below was a sheet of white, the black rocks now hidden, the zigzag path that had stepped gently down the hillside now buried beneath snowdrifts. She plunged, headlong, following a series of narrow ledges zigzagging down. Jutting rocks provided handholds.

In fresh snow beside the stream she found a footprint. Bending double, she ran her hand around its rim, imagining his tiny foot. As she looked up, she saw another footprint. A line of them extended alongside the stream. She cried out with relief. Now she would find him, wrap him in her arms, smother him in warm kisses. She would carry him back up the mountainside, past the hotel, and she and Francis would drive away, winding down the mountain road, crossing the blue, moonlit plains, not looking back and not stopping until they were home in their two-room flat, where she would tuck him in to bed, kiss him goodnight, and tell him a story.

She followed his footprints around pinnacles and between spires of jagged rock, the snow falling ever more densely. Her legs became weary as they sank in to soft snowdrifts. The wind echoed hallelujahs across the valley and struck her face with flecks of ice. Finally, she squeezed through a gap between two spires and found herself in the grotto. Straight ahead, the waterfall glistened pure and clear, like glass, like light.

Around the edges of the grotto were eight statues. Jan ran to the newest and slumped beside it, running her hands over its face, stroking its hair, wiping ice-tears from its wide, crystal eyes. She pressed her lips to the boy's, nestled her cheek against his and wrapped her arms around him so the two were one. A few tears fell from the white pupils of her eyes, but soon they hardened into tiny icicles. Frost formed on her ears and nose. Soon it spread to cover her whole body, forming a thin layer of ice, densely webbed with thin cracks. For a few moments she continued to stroke Francis' hair, until her skin hardened into a clear, gleaming shell and she could no longer move her hands.

Then, she nuzzled her face in close to his. Her last heartbeat pumped freezing water into her arteries, sending pain through her stilled limbs. Her last tear crystallised just below her left eye. Her last breath formed a powdery coating of white mist on Francis's cheek. And, finally, the corners of her lips curled up to form the saddest, sweetest smile.

River Story

From the front window of my home I can see, almost hidden between the outlines of buildings and the contours of hills, the meanest view of water. It is no more than a postage stamp, a square inch on the pane. If I hold a thumb at arm's length I can obscure it completely. By day, though it sparkles, it is lost amid reflections of glass and steel. But at night the buildings lose their shine. They merge with one another, are lost in the darkness. Sky and land reflect each other in a canvas of empty blue. Then, the little patch of sea stands out. Moonlight sinks into its depths. It glows. I imagine I can see the pale tip of each rising wave, the shadows and contours of the ocean's surface.

That, at least, is how it was last night, when I sat for an hour or so in the living room, looking out that window. My son was on my knee. I told him about Helen, who I had seen that afternoon, for the first time in nine years. I felt I had to tell him, though he is too young to understand. Most of all, I just wanted to sit with him, to have him fall asleep surrounded by my warmth, with the sound of my voice in his ear.

Helen and I were taking a walk in a park. It was late afternoon, in the middle of winter. The sun was low and pale. Soft, anaemic shadows spread over everything.

We walked, hand in hand, along a path under a line of oak trees, all silver and bare, with twigs growing in fans from the tips of their branches.

I felt her hand tighten its grip.

'What's up?' I asked.

She didn't say anything. Her skin was pale, her eyes downcast. She bit her lower lip.

We walked on, past a garden of spindly rosebushes, past the grey riverstone walls of the art gallery. A narrow path led to the river. The last, fallen leaves, red and rotting brown, crunched under our feet. Some blew into the water, rippling its green, glassy surface. I watched them flow downstream, around a bend. As each leaf disappeared I felt something—a kind of regret—but then another leaf caught my eye. Each was different: one long and thin, another broad, another curled up tight.

'I like rivers,' I said.

Helen frowned.

I had been going to say how I liked the way rivers moved—like time passing—and I liked that the water they carried might some day end up falling as rain, perhaps here, perhaps somewhere else altogether.

Instead I asked, 'What's wrong?'

She let go of my hand and took a step away from me.

Rain, on cue, began to fall. It pattered very lightly on the leaves and broke the river's surface with tiny spots.

Helen walked off.

'Wait for me,' I said.

She turned towards me.

'Can't you keep up?' she said. 'Can't you do something right?'

I stood still, letting the rain form a light skin on my hands and face and clothes, and watched her walk under the shadows of the oaks, along the curve of the river, until I couldn't see her any more.

Then I ran to catch up.

When I reached her, I tried to put my arm around her. She shook it off.

'I don't want that,' she said.

'What *do* you want?' I asked. 'Should I go away? Do you want me to go?'

Her eyes were suddenly glassy. She shrugged.

'No,' she said. 'I don't. I just didn't know how to tell you. I'm pregnant.'

That night, in bed, she lay with her back to me. I leaned towards her, placing a tentative hand on her shoulder. When she didn't respond I moved closer until my body was curved against hers. I moved my hand on to her belly, allowing it to rest there, and I curled my legs against hers. I felt her go tense. She clicked her tongue, sighed, rearranged her pillow, and moved as far from me as the bed allowed. I watched the rise and fall of her back, a blue continent outlined by a faint glimmer of moonlight. The space between us was an ocean, uncrossable. I turned away, closed my eyes, tried to imagine reaching down into a crib, picking up a baby, cradling its head in my palm, gazing into its dark, unfocused eyes—but I couldn't hold on to that picture. I saw only darkness, the moonlit outlines of clothes draped over furniture, the dim glow of the glossy white door.

When I look back now, I wonder if it was then she decided. As we lay together in the darkness, did she sense my weakness, my sentimentality? Did the whiff of it drift over to her, gather under her nose so she could inhale it? As she breathed it in, did she understand that I would make no decision except to wait?

In the morning I was woken by sharp sunlight. Helen's side of the bed was empty. I placed my hand on the sheets where she had been. For several minutes I stayed there, nestled against her warmth, feeling lost, frightened, sorry for myself.

When I got out of bed, I dressed in old jeans and a jumper that was full of holes. I found Helen in the kitchen. The jug was boiling, filling the room with steam. The benches and cupboards glinted with condensation and the bottom half of the window was fogged. I switched the jug off and took Helen in my arms. As she raised her face to me, her tears brushed my cheeks and ran on to my neck, under the jumper's round collar. I don't know how long we stayed like that, but it felt like a long time. It felt as if the earth had turned full circle. I have always grieved for that lost day.

'Did you sleep?'

She shook her head. Tiny wrinkles had formed under her eyes.

'Thinking,' she said, tapping a finger against the side of her head. 'Thinking, thinking.'

Anything I said could push us towards a decision, so I said nothing. But her eyes were searching my face. They were wide open— dancing, skimming. She seemed to be holding out her whole body to me, arching it up so our faces were almost level.

'Thinking what?' I asked.

She had wanted me to catch the weight that was falling towards us, hold it out to her, show her it was small enough to contain in the palm of a hand—it was a bead of glinting water, a jewel— but I stood, helpless, as it fell.

'You don't know anything,' she said. 'You don't know the first fucking thing.'

She left the room. I heard her bare feet on the floorboards, and the gentle click of the bedroom door. I went outside. It was a bright, clear day. A girl was going past, walking a dog. It was a big dog, a St Bernard, pulling on its lead, and the girl was struggling to hold it. As she passed, she looked at me and I felt as if I should help, but something held me back. Soon, the dog sped up and the girl was forced to run. They turned a corner and disappeared. I kept watching the space where they had been, thinking I saw them against the houses at the end of the street.

When I turned to go in, Helen was coming down the path towards me. She was dressed in a sweatshirt and jeans and a pair of running shoes.

'Come for a walk?' she said brightly.

She took my hand and led me down the street, past rows of villas identical to the one she rented— once-proud, with grand entrances and wide bay windows, but by then dilapidated, waiting for demolition. They are probably all gone now. Near the end of the street two had already been pulled down to make way for townhouses. We cut across the empty section and came out on another street, narrow and treeless, lined with the dull, grey frontages of low-rise office buildings and wholesalers. Between two of those buildings was a narrow lane, deep in shadow. A sliver of bright sky was visible above.

'Where are you taking me?' I asked.

Helen put her hands on my shoulders and pulled herself up. I felt her whispered breath in my ear.

'Trust me.'

The end of the lane opened into a service alley, lined with rubbish bins and cars parked at skewed angles. Helen climbed on to one of the bins. I watched the sinewy curve of her body as she stretched up and caught the lowest rung of a fire escape ladder. Blood rose in her face as she began to climb. When she reached the first landing she looked down and said, 'Well? Are you coming or not?'

When I reached the platform she wrapped her arms around my neck and kissed me, then turned and began to climb—up another ladder and another, until we stepped on to the roof. The city we lived in was built on a plain, with wide streets that went on forever in straight lines and buildings that looked out on nothing but each other. The only views were from rooftops.

A low concrete wall ran around the edge of the roof. Helen climbed on to it and began walking, her arms spread wide for balance.

'Coming up?' she asked. 'It's fun.'

I was terrified she would fall, though her movements were smooth and liquid, in gentle arcs. With each step she landed soft and sure on the balls of her feet. Her limbs seemed to give a little on impact.

I shook my head.

'You're so scared.' She did a little skip. 'You're scared of everything.'

I took a step closer, reached out a hand. She began to run. My mouth opened and my throat burned—but I had nothing to say, nothing to bring her down.

'Will you marry me?' she said.

I nodded.

'Shall we keep it?'

Her voice was songlike, taunting. Mine was a whisper.

'Yes.'

She jumped. I felt a rush of air against my skin. Something struck my face and chest. I fell backwards and landed hard on the roof.

'That was clumsy,' she said.

I opened my eyes and saw her beside me: green eyes wide open, auburn hair falling across her face. She moved towards me as if she was going to kiss me, then her head slumped against my chest. I touched my fingers to her face. Her eyes were perfectly still, staring beyond me, beyond the ledge of the roof.

'Are you okay?' I asked. 'What can I do? Helen?'

She sat up and looked at me.

'Look at this,' she said, springing to her feet, pulling me up by the hand. Together, we leaned against the perimeter wall and looked down over the city. Below us was a line of squat, concrete buildings and toylike cars and stunted trees. A little further off was the city centre, with its few glimmering towers of glass and steel, reflecting the cloudless sky. Beyond that was a tic-tac-toe of long, straight, wide suburban streets, all lined with houses on little rectangles of land. These sections were dotted with trees—pines, lush with oil-black foliage, and willows and birches, pale and naked. In the distance, the city gave way to a plain of golden farmland, which in turn yielded to a thin, blue coastline.

Snaking through this whole scene was the river, its surface licked with orange flames reflecting the afternoon light. It appeared beneath the oak trees in the park and flowed across the city, disappearing behind the high-rises and reappearing between the suburban homes. When it reached the plain, it split into a dozen branches, and each of them fanned into a dozen more, until it was no longer a river but a family of streams, a parent and its children, all running together, out towards the hazy blue line where sea met sky.

'You say the right things,' she said. 'But you don't mean them.'

By the time we had retraced our steps, down the fire escape, through the lane, across the section, along the street to Helen's flat, the sun was beginning to set, a soft breeze was rising, and there was nothing left to do but make the arrangements. That night we ate pizza and drank beer and lay on the couch in Helen's living room. We watched a nature documentary on TV about a lioness trying to teach her cubs to hunt. The cubs kept wrestling on the ground and making little mewing noises while the lioness growled and snatched at them with her mouth, trying to pull them apart. They were the cutest things, with ears soft as butterfly wings and eyes full of mischief.

The next day Helen saw a doctor, and the day after that she had an appointment at the clinic. Over those two nights I didn't sleep. I lay beside her in the half-darkness, memorising her: almond eyelids which flickered as she dreamed; skin, chalk-coloured in the moonlight; small mouth with soft lips; hair, falling in thin tassels over her face. Sometimes I thought, or began to say, 'We don't have to do this.' But I caught the words in my throat. I knew if I said them she would turn away, curl herself up tight, show me the hard curve of her back. I knew I would lose her.

*

My silence was worth nothing. A few weeks later, Helen came to me and told me all the things she had held inside during that time: that I was useless, that I could have helped her but I didn't. She told me she never wanted to see me again, so I left. I moved cities, found a job, put her out of my mind.

I had thought I had forgotten her until yesterday. It was late afternoon, rush hour., and I was on my way to my job in a hotel kitchen when I saw her. She was in the passenger seat of a car stopped at the intersection of Mayoral Drive and Queen. The car was two lanes away but I saw her through the open window. Her hair was darker, a brownish-black, and it was cut short and spiked with gel—but her face had not changed; she still wore the same, hard expression. She was dressed in a black jacket with pinstripes. The driver—was it her husband, I wondered? Or a lover? A friend? A workmate?—was clean-shaven, greying. He wore a dark suit. As I watched, she got out a cellphone and punched in some numbers and began to talk. 'Helen!' I called. She lifted her head and looked towards me but her expression didn't change. She kept talking on the phone. I called again, and waved, but the lights changed and the car moved off.

When my shift ended, I walked down the great, dull expanse of Hobson Street until I reached the waterfront. I sat on a pier, dangling my feet over the water, and looked out towards the black hills across the harbour. Light rain was falling, but the night was warm. I kept thinking of Helen, of what she must have been thinking at the moment she saw me. It was so like her to maintain a straight face, to pretend I wasn't there.

At first, I tried not to cry—I told myself she wasn't worth my grief. But, after a while, I let it go, allowing the tears to pool in my eyes and run down my face, into the corners of my mouth. I wasn't crying for her, but for myself—for my smallness, my meanness and lack of courage. I was crying for the child I had lost, a child I didn't even have a name for, couldn't even call 'him' or 'her', didn't have a single memory of that I could unwind from my memories of Helen.

When I got home, at about three in the morning, I checked on my wife, who was sleeping. I went to Jonno's room and gathered him, blankets and all, out of the crib. His dark eyes flickered open and he yawned silently. I carried him into the living room and settled into an armchair, cradling him in my arms. I looked out, through the window, at the sharp outlines of high-rise buildings and the tiny harbour view between them, and as I gazed at this scene, I rocked Jonno back and forth, telling him about my day, about Helen, about all the things I wished I had known before he was born. I told him he made everything all right and he stared at me as if he was trying to understand. His tiny nose wrinkled. His dark eyes were unblinking. As I held him, looking at his beautiful face, I hummed a lullaby, slow and melancholy. After a while, he yawned again and brought a tiny hand up to his mouth. He blinked and smiled. I rocked him back to sleep.

The Mandevilles

It's strange how life can turn on the smallest of things. An action or event that seems innocent at the time can lead to more than it should. For me, everything changed because of a feud with the boy next door, a rainstorm, and something to do with a fish pie.

The year was 1985. I was 16 years old, that time of life when I was beginning to have adult hopes, but retained a child's sense of how to achieve them. We had just moved into a new subdivision on the edge of town—my father, my mother, my sister and me. Labour was in office, which had made my father, a union delegate in the local meatworks, and a Pollyanna at the worst of times, even more optimistic than usual. My mother, who was saner and therefore weaker, mustered only feeble protests as he paid the deposit with his visa card.

The day we moved in was the hottest of February. As we drove down our new street the windows of the houses greeted us with blinding reflections of the sun. Our new home was slightly smaller than the rest, but still far grander than the railway house we had lived in before. It stood, squat and proud in clinker brick and decramastic tile, on a cracked brown yard where the lawn had not taken.

'Here it is,' my father said, as if only he could see what was standing before us. 'Our castle. Our new life.'

My mother made a hissing sound.

That afternoon, the boy from next door, attracted my attention by leaning over the fence and whistling.

'Hello,' he said, extending a hand casually. He was smaller than me, with a chinless face and a dark, bumfluff moustache. 'Nice day,' he said, withdrawing the hand as I reached for it.

'Suppose,' I said.

My sister came over. Graeme reached over the fence, shook her hand.

'Graeme's the name,' he said, smiling. 'Graeme Mandeville.'

I followed his eyes as they traced the outline of her sweatshirt, her ripped blue jeans. She was younger than me, by about eighteen months, and I felt protective towards her. When Graeme invited her to visit, I followed.

The Mandevilles' house was like nothing I had seen before. It was huge, for a start. Our home could have fitted snugly inside the entrance hall. It had a games room with a bar in it, and two living rooms—one for adults and another for children with a TV set that covered most of a wall.

'Drink?' Graeme asked, as he showed us the view through the ranch sliders, to the swimming pool. His sister, Amanda, was lying beside it, sunning herself in a black swimsuit.

'Sure,' I said. 'What are you having?'

'None of your business,' he said, glancing at me briefly before turning to my sister. I saw their eyes meet, something catch, like a match lighting.

'Do you know what a gooseberry is?' my sister asked, after Graeme had left the room. 'Couldn't you piss off?'

I shrugged, looked out the door towards the pool. Amanda had gone. Soon Graeme returned, holding two glasses. They looked as if they were filled with coke, but I could smell the liquor as he passed.

'Here,' he said, handing one to my sister.

He turned on the TV and he and my sister sat close together on the couch. I excused myself and left.

The following day was our first at a new school. Graeme and I were both in the fifth form. In the lunch break I saw him on one of the playing fields. I picked up a stone and tossed it at him, narrowly missing his head. He was waiting when I got home and pelted me with chestnuts as I walked up the front path. Red, stinging welts formed where they struck on my legs. I retaliated with a handful of gravel from our driveway—the only unpaved one in the street.

Later, as I was watching TV, a coke can came sailing through the open window and struck me on the shoulder. I went to the freezer and fetched one of Mum's fish pies, which I carried outside and lobbed over the fence. I heard the dish shatter on the Mandevilles' front path. When I returned to my seat in front of TV, my sister shot me a glance. She went outside and I saw her talking to Graeme over the fence. I turned back to the television.

After the programme had finished, I went to my room and sat on the bed, looking across towards the Mandevilles' house. A light came on in one of their rooms and I saw Amanda come in. She dropped her schoolbag on the bed and came to the window, resting her elbows on the sill and looking out, pensively. There was a chestnut tree outside her window and she stared into its branches. Then, she looked towards my window, smiled, and closed the curtains.

The following afternoon, while I was supposed to be doing homework, I kept glancing across, looking into the empty room: Amanda's desk, piled with books; her unmade bed; her silk dressing gown hanging behind the door; a poster of Simon Le Bon on the wall above the bed. I lived, from then on, for glimpses of her. Sometimes I saw her working at her desk, or lying on her bed, reading. I watched her talking with one of her girlfriends, her golden throat rippling as she tipped her head back to laugh. Another time, she came to the window in her swimsuit, the one she had worn the first time I saw her. I watched as she reached her long arms up over her head, stretched and yawned.

She became my refuge from the battles that had broken out all around me. Things had turned sour at the factory. Dad's hours had been cut, he couldn't pay the mortgage. Mum had to find a part-time job on the checkout at Woolworths. One night, she served Dad's dinner straight on to his lap. He just sat there, his head slumped into his hands. Steaming mutton stew dripped from his legs on to the linoleum.

At the same time, things were becoming serious between my sister and Graeme Mandeville, and she abandoned her neutral stance in our battle of chestnuts and fish pies. One afternoon, she got me in the belly with a stone—a bright, flat disc that came spinning out of the air like a flying saucer. While I was bent over from the pain she stole my schoolbag and gave it to Graeme, who threw it in the Mandevilles' incinerator, library books and all.

I retaliated with a balloon-bomb of blue clothes dye which wobbled through the air, missing them both and spreading its contents over the imported marble flagstones of the Mandevilles' courtyard. My sister told my parents I had initiated the attack, a lie that caused much tutting on my mother's part, while my father winked at me. He and I were both sent to our rooms without dinner. That evening, my heart nearly broke: Amanda Mandeville left the curtains open as she changed out of her school uniform.

The next morning, on my way to school, it rained for the first time in weeks. The first drop landed smack-bang in the middle of my nose, a big, fat, juicy spot. Before long, I was drenched from head to toe. After weeks of heat the rain was soft and cool on my face. It tasted sweet as it ran into the corners of my mouth. The rain continued throughout the day. By mid-afternoon, when I left school, the streets were coated in a silvery sheen. Close to home it was knee-deep and ran with a slow current. I sloshed through it, my swollen shoes kicking aside debris.

Our front door was locked. No-one answered my knocks. The lights were off, but I could see, through the window, a shallow pool of water lapping against the furniture. I went next door, to the Mandevilles'. The water was up to their top step. I rang the bell and Amanda answered.

'Hi,' she said.

'Hi, I'm from next door. I'm locked out.'

She looked me up and down.

'You'd better come in, then.'

She stood aside and I followed her down a hallway, into the kitchen. It was a large room, with a table at the centre.

'Have a seat,' she said. 'I was just about to have a drink. Would you like one? You must be freezing.' She touched my sleeve as she asked. I had never seen her so close up. She looked different somehow. Softer, more real. Perhaps a little less pretty than I had imagined from behind my periscope.

'I'm Amanda,' she said, 'by the way.'

'I know. Ethan.'

She handed me a mug of cocoa and sat down beside me. We drank in silence. I looked at the creased cotton of her shirt and wanted to reach out and hold it between my fingers, just to feel its softness.

'You're soaking,' she said. 'I think you should get out of these wet things.'

Before I could answer she had taken me by the wrist and was leading me down the hall. She opened a door and I saw, afresh, the inside of her room: her bed, her desk, her dressing gown; Simon Le Bon, his bleached curls ten times' life size.

'You get changed,' said Amanda. 'I'll put your clothes in the dryer.'

She left the room and reappeared a moment later with a towel. I had already taken my shirt off and I saw her gaze move up and down my torso.

'Is there anything I can change into?' I asked.

She shrugged.

'Maybe I could find something of my father's.'

Her eyes searched my face. They were so beautiful, so pitying. I stepped towards her, took her hands in mine, tried to kiss her. She pulled away and looked at me, wide-eyed, motionless. I, too, was paralysed, wishing I could step back in time, unwind the moment, just disappear.

'Here,' she said, holding up the towel. 'You'd better use this.'

I reached for it with a shaking hand. As I began to wrap it around my waist Amanda pointed at me.

'What's that?'

I looked down.

'What?'

'That,' she said, pointing.

She touched the skin of my stomach, making me wince.

'It's nothing,' I said. 'Just a bruise.'

She put her arms around me. One of her hands cradled my head, pulling it in to her shoulder. The other cradled my back. She held me tightly, my skin against the cotton of her shirt. Though I had dreamed many times of being in that room, of embracing her, of feeling her hands on my skin, all I could do was fall limp against her and cry like a child.

There's not much more to tell, except that this is a story of faint hopes, of illusions. After I had cried myself out, Amanda went to her father's room and fetched me some clothes. She left me alone to dress, then invited me down the hall to watch TV. When the rain had eased and my clothes had dried, I went home and found my mother and father arguing over ruined carpet, watermarks on wallpaper.

That night, the Mandevilles came over. My mother brought out the crystal glasses and my father poured out wine and they shut themselves in the living room, despite the sodden carpet. From my room, down the hall, I heard my mother's only record, Dean Martin, playing scratchily, and after a while I heard raised voices and hands thumping on the coffee table. At first I feared it had something to do with me. I lay in the darkness, waiting for a knock on the door.

But it turned out to be my sister who was in trouble. While I had been humiliating myself with Amanda, she had been with Graeme in the Games Room, putting the ping pong table to a use the Mandevilles had not foreseen when they bought it. Somehow, they saw this as my sister's fault, and wanted an apology, along with our rapid departure from the neighbourhood.

They didn't have to wait long. When the insurance money for the carpet came through, Mum and Dad spent it on a caravan. Soon afterwards, when Dad was laid off from the factory, they sold the house.

'Here we go,' Dad said, as we pulled out of the drive for the last time. 'Off to a new life, a better life.' He grinned at me. We lived for about a year at a campsite at the beach, Mum and my sister in the caravan, Dad and I in a tent outside, before my sister moved out. I followed soon afterwards, moved back into town, signed up for the dole.

That was years ago. Not long after, I made my peace with Graeme Mandeville. We became mates, of a sort—back-slapping and rugby talk. I still see him every now and then, birthdays and Christmas, that sort of thing. It's the least I can do. He's the father of my sister's children, after all. He misses them, too—still thinks they might come back some day. I haven't the heart to tell him he's wrong. They like it in Australia.

Mum and Dad are still in the caravan in the park at the beach. The old tin heap has rusted through now. Lupins and daisies are growing around it. Dad moved in from the tent after I left. He and Mum have got nothing left but each other, and they're happier than ever.

And me? I followed in Dad's footsteps and found a job in a factory. Until recently, I was a delegate in the union. But I got laid off last week, along with everyone else. The company is moving to Korea. The whole town is dying. Only ghosts live here now. But I try to look on the bright side, to think like my father would. There'll be other jobs, other places to live. There'll be a caravan somewhere for us. There'll still be dreams, memories, stories to tell. We'll be okay, Amanda and me. We don't need anything but love.

You Make a Life

1.

My mother phoned to tell me the news. Kevin answered and she thought he was me. She was crying, he told me. She said, 'Hi baby, I've got some bad news. Daddy's died.'

'I'm very sorry,' Kevin said. 'Excuse me. Mark's not here. I'm Kevin. I'm his friend.'

He went to the door of the cabin we had rented for the weekend and looked outside. I was in the distance, walking along the beach. He went back to the phone and said again he was sorry.

'I'll get him to call you as soon as he comes in. I promise. How are you?'

My mother said, 'You're his friend?'

'Yes.'

'That's good,' she said. Kevin could hear her breathing. Then she said, 'Can you tell him it was quick in the end—it was as if he'd decided. Do you know what I mean? He went in his sleep. The doctors said he wouldn't have felt anything.'

She said 'decided' slowly, sounding it out. De. Ci. Ded. As if she had rehearsed it.

'He'll call straight away,' said Kevin. 'We'll fly over tomorrow.'

She said she would make the funeral Tuesday. It was Saturday.

When I got back to the cabin, Kevin was waiting for me. He came down from the steps and took me in his arms and told me about Mum's call. He repeated every word of it, even the pause after she said 'That's good.' He led me up the steps and into the cabin, and handed me the phone. He brought me a chair. I called my mother and she told me how Dad had slipped away in the night— so the hospital had told her.

'I should've been there,' she said. 'I was with him yesterday.'

She didn't cry this time, but she sounded short of breath.

'You did all you could, Mum,' I said. 'He couldn't have wanted anything else. Are you okay? Is someone looking after you?'

I listened to her talk about how she had nursed him until he was too sick and had to go into the hospital, how she saw him every day. I said it would be good to see her. I said I would look forward to it.

Afterwards I went and sat with Kevin on the sofa. He put his hands on my shoulders and pulled me towards him, burying my head in his chest. With one hand he stroked my hair; with the other he rubbed my back in the way my mother used to. I closed my eyes. He rocked me back and forth, back and forth. I breathed the bark smell of his skin. He made me feel safe.

'You could tell me about him,' he said.

In the thin light of the cabin, with its pale wood floors and white walls, as the sun dipped towards the horizon and came through the shutters in pink stripes, and the air, which had been hot and dry and difficult to breathe became cool and sweet, I cried, and I thought about my father, and sometimes I found things to say about him.

'I should have gone back,' I said. My tongue curled under the taste of salt. 'I had known for ages. I didn't go back.'

I told Kevin about the last time Dad and I had spoken, which was six months ago, almost to the day. I had counted. Dad had phoned me when he found out.

'Mark,' he said. A command.

'Yes?'

'It's your father, you fool.' He sounded so old. Each word was punctuated with catarrh. He was a pack-a-day man.

'Dad.'

He told me he was dying. I waited for him to continue. I had nothing to say, not even then. It was the same all my life—not saying anything in case what I said was wrong.

'Well, say *something*,' he said. 'Say it serves me right if you want.'

I asked him what the doctors had said and he told me.

'It's inoperable,' he said. 'It's all over me. I've got two or three months left, maybe four. Six at the outside.'

I didn't know what to say. I just held on to the phone. I could hear the pulse in my ear.

'Look,' he said. 'I don't suppose I'll see you again.'

I heard him breathing.

'I want to say, I don't know anything about you, never have. I don't understand you. But I hope you're happy.'

At the time I wasn't happy, but I told him, 'Yes, Dad, I'm happy.' Lost for anything else to say I added, 'I hope you're happy too.'

He seemed not to hear that.

'I'm sorry for everything,' he continued. 'I hope I haven't been too bad a father.'

'No,' I said. 'You haven't.'

'I could have said he was good,' I told Kevin. 'Would that have hurt me?'

Most of my memories of him are like snapshots—
ones taken from odd angles or with thumbs in the
way or dark shadows across people's faces or things
sticking out from behind their heads, the kind that
get left out of albums, tossed in boxes that are
hidden away in cupboards. They are simple images,
like the view of his chin when I was sitting on his
lap, with its dimple and its hundreds—no,
thousands—of tiny black spots where, though he
was clean-shaven and his skin was soft, hair was
waiting to grow; his nakedness in the changing
sheds at the public baths, which was a shock to me
because his body was slim and milk-smooth, yet in
his jeans and leather jacket he seemed muscular
and hard; the cigarette smell when he came into
my bedroom to say goodnight, which made me
hold my breath and turn away; him walking down
the drive away from the house, his overalls
ballooning at his waist, and the way he faltered
mid-stride, when his knee seemed to lock up and
his leg froze in mid-air; his eyes, bare slits of
marble-white; his delicate lips, too pink and pencil-
thin for a hard man; his black-clad leg arcing
towards the kick-starter of his motorbike.

He and I were opposites. I inherited Mum's
heavier build and softer manner. Even as I loved
him I knew I would never resemble him in looks or
ways. In their many rows and fragile truces, I sided
with Mum, hiding behind her cotton skirts and
once, perhaps twice, standing in front, getting my
body between them, in a show of boyhood bravura

(perhaps I resembled him just a little). He never hit me, and never hit her as far as I know, but his rage was an aura around him, it made him bang doors and bump into things. He shouted and threw glasses, plates, knives and forks—not *at* us but at walls and windows and unoccupied chairs *near* us.

I remember him outside, working on his bike. An old towel lay on the ground and grease-covered engine parts were laid all over it, along with a red tin containing his socket set and a black case with other tools. Some of his friends were there—a man with a too-small T-shirt that didn't cover his belly (a hairy globe that seemed to float in the air before him) and a woman who was short and drainpipe-skinny, with a long velvet dress on. All three were drinking beer while Dad fiddled with his bike, taking things off, putting them on. I watched from a window. Hairy Man was standing close behind Stick Woman, pushing at her, with his hands on her breasts. As he stood there he chatted to my father, saying 'Should've seen me go, smooth I was, and fast,' and 'Saw the new Ducati the other day in Morrison's. Ooosh!' While I was watching, my mother came into the room and looked out the window and said, 'You shouldn't stare at people like that.' 'Mum,' I said, 'do you like those people?' She backed out of the room, saying nothing. Some time afterwards I went outside. I stood for a while, watching them, until Dad said. 'What are you doing?'

'Nothing,' I said. 'Just watching.'

'Go inside,' he said.

'No.'

'Do what you're told,' he said.

'No,' I said. 'You can't tell me anything. You aren't even really my dad. Mum had it off with someone else.'

I expected him to be angry, to pick up a wrench or something and throw it at the house, to yell at me, but he just crumpled to his knees and looked away from me. I didn't believe it at the time. It was just something I'd made up. Maybe I'd wished for it. I found out years later it was true. My father married her for pity, and because he wouldn't have got anyone else. They made the life they could, under the circumstances, according to the rules of the time. I was the fruit of their compromise. I belonged to him, not by birth, but by experience.

Another time, one Friday night, Mum got called out to work. Dad was at the pub. She left me with a plate of stew to heat up and told me, 'Under no circumstances let anyone in.' It was the day after my birthday. Dad had given me a box of cars. I didn't much like cars but I spent the evening playing with them and listening to the television. Sometime around eleven the doorbell rang. I went out into the hallway and saw his face pressed against the smoked glass.

'Lemme in, boy,' he said. 'I forgot my keys.'

I went to the door and reached for the handle, then pulled back.

'I can't,' I said. 'Mum said don't let anyone in.'

'What d'you mean?' he said. 'I'm your Dad.'

He hit the glass with his fist. The door shook and I thought it was going to break.

'You're my Dad,' I said.

'So you can let me in,' he said.

I didn't answer. I had already told him.

'Well, fuck that,' he said. He kicked the door.

'Where is the bitch?'

He was not a bad man. He was ordinary. He needed my mother and me, and resented us just as much. These things I told Kevin.

I also remember him standing in a doorway, a bright, burning sun making a brown shadow of him. I remember being woken by his hands soft on my shoulders and being surprised by his kiss on my forehead. I remember the gifts he used to bring me —black T-shirts with pictures of motorcycles on them, socket wrenches, screwdrivers. I loved him, and now he has gone.

2.

Sunday. I overslept while Kevin cleaned up the cabin, paid the bill, and loaded the car. Now he is driving me to Sydney, to the airport. He says he will come with me across the Tasman.

I watch his hands on the black leather of the wheel. They are beautiful, long and slender with bones that stand out like tracks in sand, and tiny blond hairs all growing at the same angle, like windblown grass. His fingers too are long, slim, with little pampas knots of hair above the knuckles, and smooth, pale skin below. The nails are neatly trimmed, and marked with tiny vertical lines and pale globes of reflected sun. I watch his hands constantly, as if looking away—at the road, the pink earth, the snaky bush which now and then gives way to glimpses of river or estuary—would be an action too careless, might lead to him being picked up by the wind and tossed away.

I met him six months, three weeks, two days, sixteen hours, and four minutes ago, give or take the seconds, on the fourteenth story of a building on George Street, in a windowless meeting room with a table of un-oiled maple and eight swivel chairs in natural leather. Seven of the chairs were occupied by strangers—potential clients—with faces as blank as dough. In the eighth, directly opposite mine, sat Kevin, dressed all in black, his shirt buttoned up to the collar. He was silent and serene, his face pale, his eyes unblinking, his elbows on the table and his hands, *those* hands, clasped together as if in prayer. I stumbled and stuttered, my tongue thick between my lips. No-one asked any questions. Most of them left behind the little folder I had so carefully prepared. When I had finished they all filed out, leaving me cursing as I stuffed my laptop and papers into their case. But when I turned to leave he was waiting in the doorway, smiling.

'That seemed to go well,' he said.

We went for a drink at one of those brash, brassy bars at The Rocks, and by the time we left, some hours later, I was devoted. I was devoted to his laugh, his smile, the serious expression he wore, the way his eyes scanned my face when he listened. He is not my first lover, but he is my first real love —the first I can miss when he leaves the room, can hold just for the sake of holding, can consider a life with.

Up ahead, clouds gather over Sydney, but here the sun is noon-high and makes everything stark. We are on a bridge over the Hawkesbury. It joins the road seamlessly and goes on for miles in a smooth curve, while below us the river is a vein of mercury in a valley of glittering stones. I look out for signs, and wonder if this will be our only trip together. I can't believe he is coming with me. When we land I will introduce him to my mother and he will kiss her cheek and say, once again, how sorry he is. He will allow me to see with fresh eyes the squat, unliberated town of my youth—its wide treeless streets, its unrelenting flatness, its rows of houses with tiny windows facing each other unblinkingly, and their dull, fenceless lawns unbroken by flowers or trees, only by water-filled bottles to keep dogs away.

He will sit in the driveway in the deckchair my father used to sit in, beside the tin garage where the bikes are rusting away. He will eat at the oak table my mother inherited from her mother. He will lie with me on the single bed where I used to lie alone, gazing up at the ceiling, wishing for some sort of deliverance—a deliverance I could not even imagine, let alone put a name to. I cannot believe it, so I ask him what he thinks, and for the briefest moment his eyes leave the road, he glances at me and says, 'I think we should turn here.' And for that irrational second I am grateful to my father. I think he has died on purpose, and left me Kevin as his parting gift.

It Gets Cold Up Here

My grandfather's farm is about an hour from the city, by the motorway at first, then on a narrow highway that winds its way through the hills, and then by a gravel road which is several kilometres long and has no other houses on it. The farm used to cover a good part of the hills from the west coast to the east, but now it's just a smallholding—a lifestyle block, the agents would say. Grandad sold most of the land twenty years ago, after Dad said he didn't want it. Grandad kept living there, with no phone and no-one for company. About a year later a farm inspector found him sitting at the table with a fork in one hand and a burnt-out cigarette in the other. He must have just died, because the stew in the plate on the table in front of him was still warm—or so I was told. I was just a boy when it happened and I don't remember it. I heard about it much later, from Dad.

'My father died of a broken heart,' Dad said. I think he meant the land. Mum and Dad kept the place even though it was run down, with a rusty roof and weatherboards rotten through. They burned everything of Grandad's—furniture, clothes—and left all the doors and windows open for weeks to get rid of the tobacco smell. It's so far from anywhere you could do that without fear of anyone breaking in.

Just past the house there are a few steps cut into some rock, then a path climbs up through a paddock where Grandad used to graze sheep, and through a stand of manuka, up to the hilltop. To the north and east are mountains, which on most days are shrouded in blue cloud. On good days you can see their white peaks, with a glimpse of the yellow plains of the east coast between them. To the south and west are foothills covered in dense bush, and a lush green plateau which stretches almost to the horizon before it gives way to a bright line of sea.

I took Lucy there once. She was silent on the drive up and I remember glancing over and seeing her hands folded together on her lap, scratching each other. I couldn't see her face because she was turned away from me, looking out the window. I wanted to reach over to her but couldn't let go of the wheel. The road was edged with cliffs—rising on one side and falling on the other. I felt an urge, as I approached a corner, to drive straight on towards the clouds. I was thinking about what it would feel like to float in mid-air, waiting for the moment when the car's forward momentum died and it began to fall. Nothing I could do, pumping the brakes or turning the wheel, would make any difference then. I pulled out just in time and swerved into the gravel. Lucy screamed. The verge was wide and there was a squat tin fence at its edge. Otherwise it would have been close.

'Sorry,' I said.

When we arrived I unloaded the bags and the picnic hamper and chilly bin and carried them into the house. I walked from room to room, opening windows to let air in. It was damp and had that mildew smell houses get when they are closed up for a long time. Lucy was in the kitchen, filling the kettle. She looked up from the sink and smiled.

'I'm just going up the hill,' I said.

She followed me outside. I heard her footsteps behind me on the gravel. I turned and faced her. She stopped. I turned away and walked around the side of the house. It had been raining and the first few steps of the pathway had washed away, leaving a small, muddy bank. I scrambled up on my knees. From there it was as I had remembered it—a narrow gorge of clay and flaky rock, stepping its way up the hillside. At the hilltop was a broad sandstone plateau, smooth as a tabletop, as if it had been sliced off in some quake or storm. I walked across it with small, careful steps, unable to see the edges because of a mist which had gathered around it. The mountains, the plains, the sea—all of the things I remembered from my childhood—did not exist. The mist coated my skin in tiny droplets of ice-cold water. I lay on my back and stared up at the mass of cloud, swirling atoms of dense, pale grey, in which each droplet was an individual cell, transparent at its centre, with a ring of silver at its edge. I must have fallen asleep because the next thing I knew darkness had fallen and the sky had cleared. It was a strange, bruised blue, marked all over with clear, sharp stars. The land was black, the sea moonlit. I could hear no sound, save the hollow whisper of waves and the answering northerly keen.

I had stayed there until nightfall only once before. When I was a boy, we went up to the farmhouse for a holiday. Grandad still had the whole farm and I spent my days exploring it. I crossed the sheep paddocks and walked down a gully where a tiny creek came trickling out of the rocks, or I followed the gravel road up and down through the valleys until I reached the highway and had to turn back. But my favourite place was the hilltop. It was close enough to the house that I could get there in a few minutes, but steep enough that no-one followed. Once I had discovered it, I spent my days there. Sometimes I took a book. Sometimes I just sat and stared at the horizon until my eyes blurred and it became a bright smear of blue-green light.

On one of those days I came back to the house and found Dad and Grandad at the table. Mum must have been in the kitchen because there was a smell of food in the air. Dad seemed angry. I went to him and tried to climb on to his knee but he pushed me away. When I went to him again he stood—he was a tall man and heavily built—and

104

slammed his fist on the table. Then he picked up his glass and threw it at the fireplace. It smashed and went everywhere, its contents hissing in the fire. Dad shouted something, then stamped out of the room, slamming the door behind him. I looked at Grandad and he looked directly back at me but didn't seem to see me—his eyes were like grey stones. He sat perfectly still for several minutes. At first I thought he was dead, but then a tear appeared in one of his eyes. He reached up a hand and wiped it away. That seemed to wake him up. He pushed his chair back, stood, and walked out into the yard.

Those few moments are my only clear memory of him. We didn't go back for years, not until after he died and Dad inherited what was left of the farm. I never found out what the fight was about. After Grandad left the house I went up the hill. At the top I found Dad, sitting on a rock, staring into the distance. When he saw me he smiled and held out his hand to pull me up the last few steps, but I didn't want to see him so I scrabbled back down, half-climbing and half-falling. I waited in the house for hours, until I heard his footsteps. He came in the front door and I left by the back. I raced up the hill as fast as I could. When I reached the top I lay on a piece of rock and watched some clouds blow past, lit up by the setting sun. The sky was amber. I watched until the last of the sun flickered and went out.

Lucy was asleep when I got back. The lights were off apart from a small lamp on my side of the bed, which filled the room with a brown glow. She didn't stir. I had slipped on the way down and was bleeding, so I went to the bathroom and stripped off my shirt. I turned on the hot tap, dabbed the end of a towel under the steaming water and patted my elbow. It stung. A flap of skin had been torn off, leaving a graze in which blood pooled. The towel soaked up the blood, and for a few moments I saw a patch of new skin, pale as porcelain, before stripes of fresh blood flowed in.

After I had cleaned myself I went through to the bedroom and knelt beside Lucy. I pulled the sheet and blankets over her shoulders, and nestled them under her chin, tucking them in tight so they wouldn't move until morning. I walked around to my side of the bed, switched off the lamp, climbed in, and tried to pull the blankets up but I hadn't left enough for myself. I moved closer to Lucy and wrapped my arm around her waist and nestled my face into her shoulder. Her breath quickened and stilled again. I lay in the darkness, feeling my own breath reflecting off her neck, warming my face. I tried to empty my mind. The last thing I thought was, 'I need to stay warm, it gets cold up here.'

I could never get Lucy to go back. She didn't like the place. It was cold and mildewy, she said, and dark and lonely, and too far from everything. She told me she'd woken in the middle of the night and couldn't get back to sleep. She felt like there was someone in the room, watching us. She got up and turned on the light to check.

'You didn't even wake up,' she told me accusingly. I laughed.

'The only ghost there would be Grandad,' I said, 'and it would be me he'd haunt, not you.'

I was joking about him, but I didn't think it was funny. I missed him, or at least missed the *thought* of him. I wished I had known him better, that I had just one photograph of him. I felt a kind of grief for the stories he could have told.

And I feel sad, now, that I don't have more to say about him. I so desperately want to do better, to give him a proper tribute, something to replace the land, since that'll be lost soon too. It's going up for auction this Saturday. I have to sell it now Lucy has gone. She gets half of everything.

Mississippi

Ray King and Paul Crawley landed in New Orleans late on a Tuesday morning after a nineteen-hour flight, all the way from New Zealand. Crawley waited for the bags while King went to the bathroom and splashed his face and hair with water. He filled his cupped hand and raised it to his mouth, watching himself in the mirror—hair messed up from sleeping through the flight; eyes dull and tired; skin pale. King had never liked his own face. Brown hair, brown eyes, a modest nose: in every way it was plain.

He heard the door swing open. Crawley walked into the room and came up behind him, met his eyes in the mirror with an accusing glare. King shifted uncomfortably and withdrew his gaze. He turned away from the sink, to a row of towel dispensers on another wall.

'You okay?' he asked, mildly. No answer came, and King turned to see that he was alone.

Ray, this is the hardest thing I have ever done. I hardly know where to start, so I'll just say it quickly and then it will be done. I am writing this down because it is so hard to talk—I never see you alone...

King stared for a moment at the empty space where he thought Crawley had been standing. 'Paul?' He saw linoleum, bright under fluorescent light, and when he looked up again he saw cubicle doors, another row of sinks, another mirror reflecting the light. 'Paul?' He knocked on one of the doors and it swung open. Someone had unrolled the toilet paper and torn it up, strewn it around the cubicle. King closed the door quickly and left the bathroom.

He found Crawley at the baggage carousel. They collected their bags and went outside into the warm, sweet air and caught a cab into the city. Crawley dozed on the seat, sweating airline whisky. King listened to the hiss of tyres on the freeway, watched the roadside billboards fly past in a blur. After a while the cab pulled off the freeway. It swung around a bend and slowed sharply. They found themselves on a narrow street, in the shadows of high-rise buildings. Crawley snored and gulped in a breath. He slowly opened one eye, then closed it again.

'Long flight?' the driver said. He was a burly man with a heavy moustache and wild eyes. King could see them in the mirror.

'Yeah, pretty long,' he said.

'Your friend a little worse for wear?'

'Yeah,' he said. 'Looks that way.'

The driver shifted in his seat. He raised a meaty hand and tapped on a sign on the dashboard: Soiling the cab: $100.

... Ray, perhaps this will come as a shock to you, I think I want to be with you. At least I want to find out. I think I have known this for a long time but I haven't let myself see it. I keep burying ...

They checked into their hotel, a dark old villa on the corner of Bourbon and Dumaine. King slept the afternoon away. When he woke, he found Crawley in the living room, watching a wrestling show on television. One of the wrestlers, dressed in an American flag, dived from the ropes on to the head of another. King looked into his friend's face: pale brown eyes; thick, grey stubble; dark, weatherworn skin. They turned off the TV, went out on to the balcony and looked along the street. All of the buildings were three storeys tall, with tangles of dark filigree growing on their balconies, all with shuttered windows. They were the colours of spices: cinnamon, cardamom, anise, lime leaf. Already, in late afternoon, sounds of piano and brass floated down the street. Crawley went inside and came back a moment later with two bottles of Corona. He handed one to King. They clinked the bottles. Crawley swallowed his half-down.

That night, they ate jambalaya at a diner across the road from the hotel, then found themselves wandering around the Quarter, up and down

Bourbon Street, carried along in a crowd. They stopped at a hole-in-the-wall and ordered two Hurricane cocktails. The vendor flicked a tap and they watched the dirty-looking yellow liquid flow down a plastic pipe from the ceiling, into milkshake-sized paper cups. King handed over a ten dollar note. The cocktail tasted sickly-sweet, like pineapple cordial or fizzy drink gone flat.

Music wafted out from bars into the warm night air—a tinkling lounge bar piano here, a rough skiffle-board rhythm there, tinny karaoke sounds from the only bar with a queue outside, and slow, old-time blues, all mingling, all unified by the pluck of bass and swing of trumpet and plaintive old men's voices coming from the jazz bars. The sky turned to a faded mauve and from there to a glossy blue-black. Bourbon Street became even more crowded. King and Crawley could hardly walk without being buffeted from one side or another.

'Hey,' Crawley yelled in King's ear. 'Look at that!'

A shirtless man, young, dark-tanned, muscular, pushed his way through the crowd. He wore a pair of white jeans and a head-dress of brown-tipped white feathers. Close behind him was another man, middle-aged, in a cowhide jacket and trousers and a white stetson, brandishing a silver pistol. When King turned away from the two men he saw Crawley walking close behind a young woman. She looked half his age, barely twenty, twig-thin, and wore a tight pink halter top that exposed her smooth midriff. Crawley tapped her on the shoulder.

'You're so beeeeauuutiful,' he slurred. 'Would you dance with me?'

King turned away from him, allowed himself to disappear into the crowd. He turned on to a side street where the crowd was a little thinner, the light a little dimmer. His ears were ringing. He leaned against a balcony post outside a bar, listened to the song floating from inside. The rhythm was slow, swaying. It made him feel so light, so happy, as if he could just float away, over the neon, over the hotels and the music. It was like waking on a still summer morning, or beside a river on a hot afternoon. It was the feeling he had from weed, when he was younger. Light, just a little sentimental...

'Hey, my friend!' Crawley's voice came out of the darkness. 'Come with me. Look what I've found.'

King turned just in time to see Crawley disappear into a doorway. King followed, through a twist and turn of darkness, along a corridor which opened out into a big, dimly lit bar. He followed Crawley to a table, sat down, looked up towards a spotlit stage in the corner of the room, where a woman was slow dancing. She was dark-skinned, broad-faced, had eyes like twin moons, and moved like a snake, her bejewelled hand sliding up and down her thighs. Her movements were smooth and sure as flowing water. She swayed her breezy hips, raised her arms over her head, swung them slowly, as if she was trying to pluck something—a bird, a leaf—out of the air. Crawley brought a beer bottle to his lips and took a sip. He swilled the bottle and put it down on the table with a thud.

'That girl,' he said, motioning with his thumb, 'reminds me of Angeline.'

King coughed.

'Really?' he said. Images of her: black hair falling over her face; spidery hands, stubbing out a cigarette; its savoury taste in the air.

'I don't see it,' said King.

'I don't care,' said Crawley. 'She reminds me, that's all I have to say.'

Crawley picked up his beer, tipped the bottle back and drained it. King took a sip from his. He closed his eyes, remembered waiting at the front window of his house, watching for her car.

'You must wish she was here,' King said.

Crawley shrugged.

'Well,' said Crawley. 'I don't know. Maybe.'

'Paul?'

'Yeah, of course. That's how I'd planned it.'

Crawley turned away from King, held his hand up and waved it.

'Hey!' he yelled.

A waitress came over. She stood with a pen poised over a notebook.

'Yeah?'

King turned back towards the stage. Another woman was dancing now. The music was louder, a pulsing dance beat. A strobe flashed on and off. King drank the rest of his beer, leaned back in his seat. He remembered walking out to the front gate, looking down the road for her—and going back in when the phone rang, picking it up, expecting her voice, but instead hearing Crawley on the other end, crying. She was dead, hit by a car. She'd been out walking. Crawley saying: 'I just don't get it. Why was she *there*? I can't figure out where she was going.' Guilt and grief mingling in King's blood, rushing into his stomach.

'I'm sorry,' King said. 'I'm just so sorry.'

'Yeah,' said Crawley.

They both turned and watched the stage.

After a while, Crawley got up from the table and went to the bar. He whispered something to the barman, got out his wallet and handed over some money. Then, he walked over to a door beside the bar and disappeared.

... my feelings but every time I see you they come rising to the surface. There are so many things I love about you. Your kindness. The look on your face just before you laugh. The way you skirt around a conversation, as if you aren't quite there. I don't know if any of this makes sense. I feel sad about

Paul, but I know it is over, no matter what happens with you and me. He isn't the man I married. You must have seen that. I don't want to say more...

Back at the hotel, King lay awake in the shadows, unable to shake off an awareness of light and sound from the street below. He stared at the ceiling fan spinning above him, its wings a blur. Despite its motion, the room was steamy, the air too still. He climbed out of bed, peeled off his pyjama shirt, which was moist with sweat. He pulled the bedcovers down and climbed back in, lying on his back. His hands rested on his belly. He felt the slick of dark hair over his belly-button, and the soft skin. Gradually, he drifted to sleep.

Half an hour later he sat up, without fully waking, and pulled the sheet over himself. He turned on to his side and lay with his head buried in the pillow. At about 4am he heard a noise from the balcony outside his room. He climbed from the bed and went outside. The street was still full of light and sound.

'Want one?'

He spun around. An orange flash lit up the darkness. He saw Crawley's face in the matchlight. Dark shadows blotted his forehead, his cheeks, his chin. Crawley handed over a cigarette.

'I danced all night,' he said, his voice gravelly.

King lit the cigarette and dragged the smoke in, feeling its heat in his throat.

'Vertical, horizontal, upside-down, you name it,' said Crawley.

He took a step forward and held his arms out, embracing an imaginary dance partner. He stepped to the left, to the right, back, spin around... He stumbled over a planter box under the balcony rail, cursed it, and continued, to the right, and back...

King turned from him, leaned over the balcony rail, watching the crowds moving up and down the street. A soft wind mingled with the chatter and music.

'I'm going back to bed,' he said.

'You do that,' Crawley called after him.

... I know this must be hard for you—you and he have been so close. God knows I've envied you sometimes. But I see you growing apart from him, just as I am. Ray, I know this is such a big thing to ask. I hope you will forgive me. I am not doing this lightly. Let me say it clearly: I love you. I think I always have. Please, Ray, at least accept that. At least let us talk...

King woke early the next morning and went out without Crawley. He went to a café and ordered beignet and coffee. A newspaper was lying on his table. He scanned the headlines carefully, as if there was something he expected to see. Deep in the paper, he stopped on a two paragraph story about a late-night murder. 'Armed men shot and killed a 29-year-old woman outside the St. Louis

Cemetery on Basin Street shortly before one o'clock this morning. Witnesses said the men had been driving down the street, firing shots at houses from their car. One of them took aim at the woman, a tourist from Great Britain, and shot her in the head. She died instantly.' King had read about the area in guide books, before leaving New Zealand. It was one of many he had planned to visit. He wondered how many paragraphs his life might be worth, what page it would make.

When he had finished his coffee, he walked around the narrow streets, noticing how quiet they were by day. He came to the closed-in lawn of Jackson Square and sat for a while on a park bench, watching people go by. In the distance, he heard the rumbling of a tuba, the hiss of a snare drum. Before long, a band appeared around the corner—forty or fifty men, wearing crimson outfits, marching in unison, playing a lilting version of 'When the Saints Go Marching In'. He watched them pass, got up from his seat, went to the French Market, where he bought an ice-cream.

That afternoon, he and Crawley took a cruise on a riverboat, the *Natchez*. They sat together on wooden seats at the side of the boat, watching the city float by. After an hour or so, the factories and houses gave way to green riverbanks. The land beyond stretched to the horizon, flat, faded green. King stared into the water, which was dense, muddy brown. It was, perhaps, a hundred feet deep, but he couldn't see an inch below its surface.

'Where are we going?' Crawley asked.

'To Chalmette,' King said. 'I read about it. It's where the Americans beat the British in the War of Independence. The Battle of Chalmette won the war.'

'Oh.' Crawley nodded. 'So.'

When the boat pulled in, King got off and followed a crowd across a broad field. They all sat under a tree while a tour guide explained how General Andrew Jackson and his troops trapped the British on a narrow strip of land between the river and a swamp—now drained to form the field they were on. King imagined the riverside dense with dead and dying soldiers, victims of buckshot and cannon fire, bleeding on the dry earth. Dying men in red and blue coats, a field strewn with petals. When he returned to the boat, Crawley was still in his seat. He didn't even glance up.

... I'll come to see you. Send me a note and tell me when, so we can start to sort this mess out. Oh God, Ray, I don't know what else to say. Just promise we can be together. Ray, please...

The next afternoon, King and Crawley stood on the faded planks of the pier. They had both been drinking beer since lunch. King looked into Crawley's rivery eyes.

'What are you thinking?' he asked.

Crawley shrugged, raised his bottle to his lips. Without waiting for an answer, King moved to his friend's side. Together they watched movements of boats on the river. The water, in shadows, was dark and shining. An empty grey barge floated by, and a trawler. The *Natchez* pulled out from the pier, its lights flooding the water as tourists moved around on board. Crawley shifted his feet and cleared his throat.

'I'm thinking about this place,' he said. He took another sip of his drink. 'I love it here. I think I'd like to stay.'

King took a breath. The air tasted of diesel. He looked down over the railing, into the water. A leaf bobbed up and down on its surface.

'Ray,' Crawley said. 'Do you ever have any regrets? Do you ever wish life had turned out different?'

King looked into the depths of Crawley's face.

'I don't know,' he said. 'Probably. I don't know.'

He moved a little along the pier.

'I kind of think, once you've done something—anything—you can't regret it. You have to live with it. You can't wish it gone.'

Crawley nodded slowly.

'I thought that would be so,' he said.

They found a cocktail kiosk and bought two sweet, cherry-flavoured drinks. King watched as Crawley drained his and ordered another, then wandered along the boards humming to himself. A little further along the river they came to a small park. In one corner a stage had been set up on the back of a truck, and a jazz band was playing in front of a small crowd. They bought more drinks from a stall and went over and watched for a while.

When the band took a break they returned to the pier and looked at the river. Thousands of little pink sunsets rippled its surface, mingling with thousands more reflections of the city lights. Three barges pulled out from a dock and floated silently, listing against the current, until they were about half-way across. They anchored in a perfect line: dark silhouettes against the mauve sky. A crowd formed at the river's edge, catching King and Crawley in their tide. Everyone looked out over the dappled water. A whisper seemed to go around the crowd, like a breeze through trees. Everyone was waiting, watching.

The last, burnt remnants of sunlight dipped below the horizon and the sky suddenly darkened. At that moment, the air was filled with a hissing sound and a flare of red light erupted from the first of the barges, rising high over the city. A moment later, a white flare erupted from the second barge. A blue flare followed. All three strands rose high, high, high, curving towards each other until they met in an explosion of glaring bluish-white light, a flare, a star, a nova—which just as suddenly burned out, leaving a trail of white raindrops falling towards the river. Before long, the air was again hissing, the barges rocking back and forth, the sky an explosion of colour: a curtain of red, a fizz of blue, an arcing green rocket, a snowfall of pure, clear, white light.

King looked away from the brightness, then took a quick step backwards as he looked up again and saw a sea of green light plunging towards the pier. Someone near him screamed, then everyone broke into laughter and sighs of relief as the fireworks burnt out overhead, and the quiet darkness momentarily regained its hold. The same pattern repeated itself three or four times—flames of red, white and blue; searing balls of orange and green, falling on a crowd which stepped back, moved forward, stepped back again. Children burst into tears. Adults cried out, then broke into further fits of laughter. Each time the crowd moved, King noticed himself drifting further and further from the river as others pushed forward. Crawley was among them, whooping and bellowing, arms raised over his head. King watched as he climbed onto the pier-side railing, turned, and scanned the crowd. Then, another curtain of light plunged towards them, the crowd stepped back in a wave and King was knocked to the ground. He scrabbled among the moving feet and legs. Someone helped him up but he staggered again. His legs wanted to give way. He realised he was drunk.

He pushed his way to the edge of the crowd and walked along the pier. When he had left the noise and crush behind, he sat down at the river's edge, resting against the railing. He opened his eyes to darkness, not knowing how long he had slept. The barges had gone, and the crowd's hum had given way to a soft breeze. Black water lapped against the pier's concrete foot. The sun was rising by the time he reached the hotel. He slept all morning and into the afternoon. He was woken by a phone call. Crawley's body had been found a little way downriver, caught up among the ropes of a fishing trawler. King went to the morgue and identified the body. He asked the authorities to contact Crawley's children, signed the consent for an autopsy and arranged for the body to be flown home.

It was late afternoon when he got back to the hotel. His flight was booked for the next morning. He had twelve more hours in America, and felt sure he would never be back. He decided to stay in the hotel room, to get ready for the trip and then have an early night. As he packed Crawley's clothes away he went through the pockets, pulling out any personal effects so he could carry them in his hand luggage. He came across Crawley's wallet, which contained a photograph of Crawley and Angeline, both smiling, both a little fisheye distorted as one of them held the camera out in front. He sat on the bed and looked at the picture for a long time.

Then, in a jacket pocket, he found a copy of a letter, hand-written, full of cross-outs: a draft. He read and reread it, wishing it gone, wishing it never written, because it explained to him what Crawley knew, how carefully planned this trip had been, and what Crawley had meant when he said, Ray, please come with me. I need you to be there. I don't know what I'll do if you don't come. Ray, please

...do this for me, and know that I will love you always.

Angeline.

The Sea as Past

On the first day of January, Jacob woke to find that the harbour had been drained of its water and filled with golden light. He stood at the window, overlooking the hooked fingers of land, the glistening high-rises, the layer of whispering clouds, all tinged mustard-brown by the strange, salty glow.

'Louise!' he called to his wife. 'Come and look at this!'

He had dived in many countries and only once, thirty years ago in a small bay on St Kitts, had he seen the sea turn gold. On that occasion the whole population, about twenty thousand people, had rushed into the warm light and swum among the schools of tropical fish, exclaiming at the miraculous, healing powers of that bright sea until, at dusk, it turned back to its usual turquoise and they drowned with great, happy gulps. He had read recently that St Kitts still had the smallest population of any country in the world, and took it as proof that diving was a branch of metaphysics and should be practised only by people who had meditated for years on the many possible meanings of salt water.

'The sea is a junk shop,' he would tell people. 'You will find bargains there, portraits and jewels from lives more glamorous than ours. It is also a menagerie—life exists there that is stranger than on other planets: there are fish with no eyes that swim in depths beyond light and reproduce by breaking themselves like coral. And it is a graveyard of course. I have seen more bones than I can remember: the bones of children, and bones made of gold and glass. All events exist simultaneously in the ocean, it is like a rock face with layers of fossils.' At this point he would usually find that his companion's eyes had glazed over and resolve to keep his thoughts to himself, but the silence would last only a few seconds before more thoughts came bubbling out, like a spring containing small fish, turning him into a baroque statue of Neptune, gushing oratorical water into a marble pool of unheard words. 'The contents of history can be found in the sea,' he would say. 'Those who want to avoid repeating the past should swim.'

The lines were clear on Louise's face, like furrows in a field. She stood in the doorway of the bedroom, trying to block his exit.

'Jacob, you are too old!' she said.

But he knew that she did not really care for his obedience, and was secretly tender for his boyish stubbornness: whether for the vicarious thrill or for more motherly reasons he could not tell, but he knew that if he did not override her protest some of the air would drain from her love and when he squeezed her next she would squeal and go limp in his arms. He needed her love to be hard, a thing to batter himself against, to bear cuts that would sting poisonously; how else could you tell that something was alive, when it was rigid and grew so imperceptibly, and whole genealogies could swim among its brightly coloured clefts and branches without once seeing it move?

Jacob balanced himself on one leg as he removed his trousers. The golden light lapped over his ankle, leaving a residue of salt spray. The light was warm, just as he remembered from the tropics; it would be like diving in bath water. He had not dived for several years and, as he undressed, splinters of apprehension pricked him above the eyes. He stood for a moment, examining himself. His skin had grown old. Its pale translucence disturbed him; its soapiness; its smattering of brown leopard-spots; its tobacco-coloured shadows and scoops of flesh; its faint, curving dunes and rippled sandscapes; these things sent him into a melancholic whirl and he stood for minutes on one leg, naked, paralysed, his wetsuit around his ankles, wishing for his own past, until he was disturbed by voices and saw that a crowd had gathered to listen to the crash of light on the shore.

'Father,' said a boy some distance away, 'do you see that crab, as big as a house? Do you taste the wind, with flakes of sugar? Do you see the colour of the water? How wonderful! How strange!'

'When you see things you cannot understand, you must refuse to believe them,' said the father.

Jacob watched and listened. He felt a shiver of disgust as the father took the boy in his arms and squeezed him. 'You think you can float,' the father said, 'but doubt will sink you.'

Jacob need not have worried about diving again. The muscles of the human body contain a memory more constant than time, a memory immune from the leakages that occur in the mind, a memory that stores every twitch of fibre, every axe-swing, every tug or expanse or unfurling, in a place so deep that light cannot reach it, and waits for unconscious signals to release each action, like a flood of hormones, into the bloodstream. As Jacob swam about just below the surface he felt this tide of memory, felt his anxiety dissipate and the blood flow faster in his veins, as his hands stretched out before him and his feet kicked just as they had when he was a child learning to swim in a shallow pool. His eyes seemed to focus more quickly as they adjusted to the dense light; the skin on his hands tightened as it was filled out by younger muscle and smoothed by the golden pressure. He was like a burnt autumn leaf, slowly rising up from waste ground, reattaching itself to the tree, and turning green.

He swam about in the shallows, among clouds of tiny, darting fish whose silver fins took on reflections of glinting gold and flashed at him, like the eyes of dancers winking from behind a tide of gauze. Other divers joined him in the current and swam past, naked and glowing; some stopping to wave to him and smile broadly, calling out greetings which were lost in the swell.

As he swam deeper, the gold darkened and took on a greenish tinge and Jacob felt himself sink into a layer of denser light, which sucked at him like treacle. Breathing became harder and his limbs were buffeted with litter: McDonalds wrappers and hubcaps, old tennis shoes and swarms of supermarket bags bloated with water, their handles like tentacles wrapping around his face until he could not see. He brushed off the bags, rubbing a little salt into the welts they left, and broke through the layer of litter, swimming deeper until he found himself overlooking the vast landscape of the sea floor. Though it was darker here, the gold still showed through, guiding his way with alternate fingers of light and shadow. Spiky hillsides stood before him, and green floodplains coloured by whorls of golden sea. He pinched his nose and blew, feeling a storm gather in his ears.

History is written by winners, he reminded himself, and floated down towards the beginning of time, past grapevines and apple trees drifting in the depths, past television sets flickering silently in the mass of light, past the wrecks of fishing boats, past a mall with a Lotto shop and a superette with cigarette signs in its window and a boarded-up post office, past a swarm of disputed statistics and a bundle of yellowing weather reports, past a social welfare office, past the jagged pieces of a torn-up ticket to London, past a haul of rusting Holdens carrying families towards the city, past some shattered bones and flecks of soil from Monte Cassino, past a swagman on a dusty road.

Two or three times on the way down he encountered himself: once as the dead man he might soon become, his skin flaccid, his eyes rolled back and his lips dried out like flakes of lemon rind; once as a young man, pressing himself on some unfortunate girl in the back seat of a rusting car; once as a child clutching his own bee-stung hand. Finally, he floated past a chopped-down flagstaff, through a vista of flax swamps and shadowy bush, around a village of wooden houses razed by fire and devoured by shuddering land and swelling rivers, past trenches and brown stains on the ground, past faces with family histories carved into them, and into the twisted landscape, the shower and splinter of rocks, the black wall of geology.

Louise sat at the window overlooking the harbour, a pot of tepid tea on the table beside her, her legs crossed, betraying impatience, watching as the golden light spilled over the rocks and sands and jetties, and lapped over the streets and flooded into basements. 'A fifty-year storm,' the radio crackled from the kitchen, static confirming what she already knew, for she had seen every storm for half a century and more, had tasted the rain of each on her tongue. Tobacco clouds whipped across the sky. Mount Victoria swooned and shuddered. It was not a fifty-year event but a fifty-three year one, for that was the length of time, with the embellishment of two months and four days, that had passed since she and Jacob had married in the chapel of a monastery she could see, now, on the hillside opposite.

She stirred her tea and wondered if she should phone anyone. 'I think you should come over,' she could say. 'It looks as if something has happened.' She had known for as long as she could remember that something *would* happen, or that nothing would, that one day he would go out and not return, and she would be left with a void to grieve. How many things he had seen on his travels, while she had remained at the window, watching; had brought up children; worked at the school; quietly gone about the business of caring; waited for him to come home and waited for his absence.

How many stories he had told, how many photographs he had brought of strange, underwater creatures, of phosphorescent planktons like life forms from other planets; of young men and women in wetsuits, wearing smiles beneath their masks; how much romance he had brought into their lives, she and the children; and yet, how much more she knew than he! How much she had divined from the veins of her hands, faint mauve rivers under the web of her skin; from the years of watching the movements and growth of the city, the ebb and flow of commerce and transport; from the life-giving scars she bore; and the taste of sweat on her upper lip when she took her morning walks.

Jacob would swim until he was tired. He would find some hillside in the seascape and follow it into a valley, into a cavern that would be dark on land and doubly dark at so many removes from the light, and even if the sea was gold he would be unable to see but would go on anyway, believing that he was bursting with something bright and new, until he couldn't remember which way was up. His skin would slacken and the tiredness would begin to show around his eyes, and sleep would settle on him.

A tear ran down her cheek. The window was misting up as a cool breeze rolled in, and the sky turned brown in night-time reflection of the sea, as if the small town which she preferred to call a city had been pressed flat and dipped in a bath until an image formed, then left to dry on a sill. She looked out at the hills opposite, the buildings of the city, the sea now fading to its usual colour. Shadows formed among its ripples. The moon turned to brass. The tea tasted of salt.

Small Details

I rented a house last summer in one of those narrow inlets north of the city where the hills plummet deep into the sea and the tide laps at the coastline like a teller of secrets. I wanted to write a story—about love, about mistakes I had made— and I needed stillness and quiet, I needed to be alone.

It was an old, solid house, with a view down a slope of long, yellow grass to the bright waves of an estuary and the black hills beyond. On my first morning there, I sat on the verandah, watching the sunrise. As the day wore on, I watched the clouds moving along at a steady pace, as if the sky was an ocean's surface seen from below and they were the hulls of ships.

I thought about Amy, who I had left behind in Wellington. I thought of her thin, white lips and dimpled chin with skin stretched tight around the bone. I didn't leave a number because the house had no phone and I didn't leave an address because then she might find me. She might turn up on the doorstep and want to be let in. She might interrupt my musings.

The previous day, when I told her I was going, she had sighed heavily.

'This is something I have to do,' I said.

'What about me?' she replied. 'Have you thought about that? Will I be here when you get back?'

'It's *for* you,' I said. 'A love story, a tribute.'

'How romantic.' She rolled her eyes. 'Where are you getting the money?'

'I borrowed it,' I said.

'From who?'

'From you.'

'Were you going to tell me?'

I shrugged.

'Do you even know what the story is about?'

'I told you, about love.'

'Yes, but who's in it? What happens?'

'I don't know. Those are just details. I'll figure them out when I get there.'

'You're not putting me in, are you?'

On my first evening at the house, I watched the sun disappear behind a crag in the west. For a brief time the sky was ablaze with red light. I stared at the scene, holding it to myself as if it was something I loved. After the sun disappeared, I was left alone in a still and starless dusk. I went inside. My notebook was lying on a table in the hallway. I picked it up, and turned to a fresh page, but I could think of nothing to write.

I kept thinking about the golden-grassed hillside and how a whole army of trees must once have stood there. I wondered who had taken an axe to the trees and split them for lumber? Who had built the house?

That night I dreamed of a farmer and his wife, young people full of hope, who had left their native country and sailed to the underside of the earth— they found hills as sharp as steeples and bush as dark as night when they would have been expecting a little English town laid out in a grid, with a church and a square at its centre and rolling meadows at its edges.

In my dream, I saw them clearing the land.

The farmer's wife had a thresher, with a rusting red blade and a handle run through with vertical cracks, which she used to beat down scrub. She was a tough, wiry woman, who bent her knees as she raised the thresher skywards, and when she brought it down her arms turned like a spinning globe. Vines were cut right through, leaving sharp, sap-filled wounds. Branches snapped. Leaves were sent flying in flocks.

The farmer, who was working nearby, saw the tan light of her movements blurring the air. 'This is hard work, my love,' he called.

When she had finished, her limbs were marbled with tiny cuts. He went to her and kissed them, taking blood and salt onto his tongue. With the touch of his lips the cuts closed together and a pale skin formed like milk skin.

After a while, she sat on the hillside and watched him raise his axe like a hammer and bring it down with a mighty force on the trunk of a pūriri tree. It struck with a ringing sound that echoed down the hillside.

The farmer grunted and wiped sweat from his forehead. The muscles of his back swelled as he raised the axe again and looped it behind his shoulder. This time the axe-head struck with a dense thud, which was followed by a sound of splintering. The tree tottered and fell, drunkenly, its trunk arcing above the hillside. It hit the earth with a sound of cracking branches, and it bounced back up and settled. The farmer glanced at his wife, who looked back with shining eyes.

In the morning, I skipped breakfast and went straight into the study, a dark room of shellacked panels and shelves filled with leather-bound books. It looked out on the hills above the house, which were bathed in brown light. I opened the notebook and began to write—small, dense characters; black ink on white paper; the words blurring before my eyes. I filled the page, turned to another, filled it too. After two hours I stopped and turned back the pages, staring at the dark lines of words— carelessly scribbled, like lines of painters' signatures. I could hardly read them, but I felt they were beautiful. I had the beginnings of a story: an outline, a ghost.

2.

One morning, about a year after he had come to this land, the farmer went out into his field. He was building a fence along the hillside just above a cliff. As he trod his way there, he saw a trail where one of his sheep had lost its footing. When he got closer, he saw its carcass on the rocks below. It had a gash across its belly. Brown blood stained the yellow-grey wool.

The wind was still blowing and the farmer's hands were slippery with rain and when he pulled his hammer from the belt of his britches the scree gave way beneath him. He took hold of a batten but it snapped under his weight and he slipped down the slope. Another batten snapped but the next one held and the wires of the fence pulled taut. He looked down at the vast grey tongue and blue-black throat of the cove beneath.

His wife was in the kitchen putting wood into the fireplace when she felt a sudden fear. She rushed to the verandah and looked down at the field, but could see only the billowing grass. Barefoot, she ran down the hillside, calling her husband's name. The wind answered with a tearful howl. When she reached him, he was half-unconscious from the pain of holding on. His eyes had rolled back in his head. She dug her toes into the earth and took hold of the fence wires and pulled like an oarsman until her fingers sliced almost through to the bones. Slowly, he rose, like a coffin raised on its ropes from a grave, until the earth's sharp angle eased and the wind suddenly died.

His wife lifted him over her shoulder and carried him back to their one-room cottage, where she lay him on the mattress. She nursed him with a cloth dipped in hot water until his eyes opened and he gazed at her. That night she held his head and tipped mint tea on to his lips. She made him a mutton sandwich, which he ate in tiny bites. He slept like a dead man but in the morning his strained muscles had regained their strength, so they went together into the field and watched the sun rise over the hillside, like a sphere of fire rising from the depths of hell.

The farmer was more careful after his fall. He left the fence unrepaired, and every few days a sheep fell into the crevasse.

'I have lost another,' he told her. 'I should repair it. I should find a way.'

'Sheep are stupid,' she said. 'Let them die.'

He was a simple man and believed everything she said, so he left the fence and allowed the sheep to die. She loved him dearly for this. She told him she would trust him to hold her dangling over the crevasse with nothing between her and oblivion but the calloused tips of his fingers.

Over the next few months the farmer cleared another field in the hills behind the house. Then he cleared the hills to the west and east. He moved his sheep into the new fields, protected by fences of wire and batten. One day he made a trip into the city and sold the trees he had felled. For weeks, he split the timber and laid it on a cart and used a horse to lead it down the gully to the estuary where a barge waited. As he led the horse back up the gully he whistled a tune and kept breaking into a run because he was so happy. His pocket was so full of guineas that when one fell out and was caught by the breeze he didn't care. He watched it float off over the crest of the hill and whistled a little louder.

When he got home, his wife met him at the door and kissed him. She said she had watched him lead the horse up the hillside and was proud of him and his work. He was a good man, she said. Many sad things happened to women who married on boats, but she had been lucky. He showed her the money and said he would buy her a dress and some books. He said he would build a house. That night they dined on roasted lamb and potatoes and beans. They read to each other from the Bible and prayed together to their Lord, who they believed wished them well. When they went to bed, their limbs grew together like ivy, arm linked with arm, leg linked with leg, belly against belly like twin trunks. Each, warmed by the other, dreamed of good things...

'I'll build something grand,' the farmer said in the morning. 'as grand as you deserve.'

As he went out to work, she stood at the window, watching his broad back disappear into the brown morning light. In the top field, he cut down more trees and spliced them into planks and beams, which he carried down the hillside on a dray.

Over the following weeks, he dug holes in the ground and hoisted in stumps of hardwood. He laid bearers as thick as his waist, and joined them with joists as heavy as his thighs, each fastened with a hundred nails. He built walls and used a horse to hoist them into place. He laid floorboards and burnished them with shellac. He polished the banister, laid bricks for the hearths, waxed cord for the windows, fitted expensive brass handles to the doors.

On the day the house was finished, he went to his wife in the cottage where she was sleeping. He picked her up and carried her across the field in his arms. She opened her eyes in a hallway of golden wood. Before her, a staircase led up to a landing and beyond the stairs was a window of ruby glass. Afternoon sun shone through it, casting a bright wedge of pink light along the floor towards her feet. He led her from room to room, making her close her eyes at each door. Kitchen, dining room, library, bedroom, nursery, washroom. Finally, he led her into the sitting room. A fire was burning in the grate. A window admitted a view of a field with scrawny grass, which rose up towards blue hills.

'I made all this for you,' he said. 'I didn't know what I was coming to when I left England behind. I'll admit I looked back more than once. But if I had known I was coming to you, I shouldn't have hesitated. I would have jumped overboard and swum to make the trip go faster. This is hostile land, but not with you in it.'

She took his hands and placed them on her belly.

'We'll have a son,' she said. 'He'll grow into a man and take over the farm. By then, it'll stretch beyond the mountains, and he'll have a staff of men, and work just for the pleasure of it. He'll see to it that we want for nothing.'

'Yes,' said the farmer. 'We'll want for nothing.'

3.

Days passed, and weeks, and eventually months. Winter came and covered the hillside in a smooth dusting of snow. The wind came from the south and curled down the hillside. I worked as fast as I could, filling pages with words, without paying much attention to how they fitted together. My notes grew like a knitted scarf, with each new square of colour taking it no closer to an end.

Here is some of what I wrote: 'Love is present in small details. It is the touch of fingertips, the moment before a kiss. It is a shy glance, a hand laid on a wrist, a step to one side to allow a stranger into a circle.'

I wrote: 'A lover of water dives into the sea. He swims away from the beach, past the headland, out towards the thin line of the horizon, until he is sure the water is so deep he could never touch the ocean floor. Then, he turns around and looks back at the land: the faded grey smudge of the beach, the clumps of toitoi, a hill covered in pine trees, a clear blue sky. After a few seconds, he tips his head back until it is covered in seawater. The salt stings his eyes, runs into his nose. His tongue tastes the flavours of all the ocean's fish. He takes a deep breath, allows the cool water to sink down his throat, into his lungs. It anaesthetises as it goes, so he feels only the briefest glimmer of pain. Soon, colours are floating before his eyes. He feels light, dizzy, as if he is drunk, as if he is floating, like one of those souls that rises over its body at the moment of death.

'But he does not believe in that. He believes in the water, in the crossing of barriers. He believes that by taking water into his lungs, he has shown love.'

One afternoon, as I re-read these notes, trying to figure out how they might fit together in a story, I thought of Amy, and wondered what her objections might be.

'Yes, love is present in small details, but not the details you have shown. Love is in a splinter pulled from a wound, a glass of water fetched in the middle of the night. It isn't there in a gaze or a kiss. And what about this other one—is it necessary to drown? Shouldn't the lover be able to breathe?'

4.

As winter gave way, the hills sprung forth with little brooks and trickling streams. They came running down the hillside from the hilltops where the snow had settled all winter and ran together with the water from spring rains. At the same time, my story dried up. When I sat at the desk, my notepad before me, the pages appeared vast, unfillable. I read back over my notes but they made little sense any more. They were a jumble of images—like memory. I tossed the notebook against a wall and left it there.

I began to sleep late into the morning, dreaming of the hillside still and windless, the sky with frozen clouds. When I woke, I stood on the verandah watching the sun pass its time of day. Then, I slept some more. I thought a little of Amy, but even she had faded. I could only catch glimpses of her: the shadow of her hand on our kitchen table, the way she wrinkled her nose when she was thinking.

I stopped writing altogether—I couldn't even drag my pen to write the date on a page. I locked the study door and spent whole days lying in bed, watching the faint flicker of the bulb in the centre of the ceiling and the growth of spiders' webs. In this way I spent two weeks, until one morning I was woken from my sleep by what sounded like footsteps in the room beneath me. I dressed hurriedly and went down the stairs with a pen in my hand, because it was the only weapon I had.

When I reached the bottom I saw a woman sitting in one of the chairs of the living room. She was facing away from me and all I could see was the brown bob of her hair above the chair's back. As I approached, she did not turn and even when I stood beside her she gave no indication that she saw me. She had a pale, narrow face and glassy brown eyes from which tears fell steadily. Her hands trembled. I stood beside her for a second or two, frozen between a wish to help her and a rising fury that she had come into the house without knocking, and I was about to take her by the wrist and demand that she explain herself when she stood and pushed past me—though I did not feel even a swish of air—and walked across the room and into the kitchen. After a moment I followed, but when I opened the kitchen door I found nothing inside save the slightest flicker of a cool breeze.

That night, before going to bed, I checked the windows and doors and found all of them latched, but in the morning when I came down the stairs the woman was there, in the same chair as the day before. Her eyes were again glassy, as if the tears came from a river that had flowed continuously throughout the night while I slept. Though I was surprised to see her I felt none of the anger I had the previous day. Rather, a feeling of sorrow overwhelmed me, as if I already knew somehow what was making her cry. I sat on a chair opposite her and watched her trembling hands and her tear-stained cheeks. Again, she acted as if she had not seen me and for a while I allowed her her silence.

'What's the matter?' I asked. 'Can I help?'

She flinched at the sound of my voice, but continued to stare at the floor. Quietly, she said: 'How could you help?'

Then, she climbed out of the chair and walked into the kitchen. Again, when I followed, I found the room empty. That night, I dreamed for the last time of the farmer and his wife. I saw him chasing his sheep up into the field behind the house and trying to hold them in as he mended the broken wires of the fence, but for every sheep he rescued a gust of wind snapped a batten and a new hole appeared, and another sheep escaped down the hillside as if it had a rope around its neck pulling it towards the welcoming mouth of the crevasse.

Every day after that, when I came downstairs in the morning, the woman was waiting in the chair in the living room. After that first day, she remained silent and appeared to not even notice me coming and going. Though her presence was an affront to my privacy, I found that I wasn't bothered. She was so mute that she could have been a picture on the wall. I found time dwindling away as I sat with her in the living room, and though neither of us spoke I felt a kind of silent comfort in her presence, like the comfort one feels in a room that is warmed by a fire. She really was startlingly beautiful. Her face was so pale and slim it gave her an almost luminous presence and her eyes were like sunlit water.

For several more weeks, despite the many hours we spent together, she did not utter another word to me. Sometimes I listened to the slow intake of her breath, and sometimes she hummed some tune I didn't recognise. Once I overheard her reciting in a hurried, whispered voice ...*heaven and earth and all things visible and invisible*... but when I put my head into the room and saw her on her knees before the fireplace she stopped immediately and didn't speak again for weeks in my earshot. At all times when we were together she maintained her gaze at some point beyond my shoulder, or out the window towards the upper field, or into the fire which I lit sometimes. It was as if, for her, I did not exist. Once or twice I grew angry and made a decision to throw her out, but I only had to look at her once to loosen my resolve. Then, I breathed deeply and allowed my eyes to follow hers, into the burning embers or the brightness of the grass in the field, and I realised that she had become an obsession for me and I could no more throw her out than cut off my own head.

Then, one day, she turned her gaze directly on me and held it until I felt as if I might be burned right through.

'Since you are spending so much time with me, I should probably know who you are,' she said.

I didn't know what else to do but to tell her.

'Very pleased to make your acquaintance,' she said, though she looked a little sombre.

She asked for my story and, over the next few weeks, I gave it to her. We sat each night in a room lit only by embers in the grate and I told her everything I knew from the time of my birth in a small country hospital in the middle of a coal-black night to the cry of magpies outside my window when I was a boy too young to know they weren't demons coming to fetch me, to the many shifts of town and city my parents and I and my brothers and sisters made as we went in search of happiness. I told her of a time when I believed anything in the world could happen if only I wished it and a time when I discovered the world was too vast for my wishes. I told her about Amy—how perfect it had been, how it had fallen apart. When I ran out of things to say I read to her from my notebook. She listened with a coy smile and attentive eyes, and when she spoke her voice was like the sound of a fantail's wings, always with another question. 'And then what happened?' 'And then?' 'And then?'

Once, I brought her weak tea in a dainty little china cup which was painted with flowers and vines, but she left it sitting at her side to grow cold.

When I asked her if she would tell me a little of herself, she brushed the air with her hand.

'That is not important,' she said. She never told me where she was from, nor how she had come to be in the house, nor where she went at night after I put the guard over the last embers and climbed the stairs to bed. She never told me her name.

One morning, when I went downstairs, I found her waiting in the hallway.

'I thought we might take a walk,' she said.

Before I had time to answer, she had opened the door and was outside on the verandah. I followed, hardly knowing what I was doing. Outside, the morning sunlight struck my eyes sharply. We walked up to the crest of the hill, then followed a path down into a gully and up the side of a taller peak. She walked with a steady stride, pushing gorse and fern aside with slow, strong movements, and when we reached the summit she turned and pointed at the contours below us— green bush, yellow field, the ocean like a bathful of tinsel, and the black hills beyond.

'This is my favourite place,' she said.

The wind was gusting violently and I could feel my feet almost being whipped from beneath me.

'Sometimes,' she said, 'after you have gone to sleep, I come up here. It becomes very still at night.'

The wind quietened as if at her command, and the sky suddenly darkened. A faint crescent moon fell towards earth. Later, as we crossed back down the hillside towards the house, the sun reappeared, turning the field blinding white. When I tried to take her hand she pulled away sharply. She walked off a little distance and stopped, with her back to me. I apologised and suggested we continue down the hillside to the broken old fence, with its palings pulled from the ground and the cliff below.

'It has a good view too,' I said. 'You can see a long way, almost as far as from where we have just been.'

She walked a few steps further away, then turned back to me, her hands clasped together before her.

'You can see too much,' she said.

The next morning, when I went downstairs, she was not in her usual chair. I checked every room in the house but could not find her. I went back to the sitting room and sat in the chair opposite hers, and waited all morning.

That afternoon, I walked every inch of the farm. I found no sign of her. In the evening, I went into the study and wrote down everything I could remember of her: the porcelain whiteness of her hands; the curve of her chin like the base of a heart; the way she stood on that hilltop, with her arms out wide as if she might leap off and plunge into the gully and swoop up again on a current of air; the shape of her back in the field as she turned away from me; the glow of her skin on those fire-lit nights. I went to bed after midnight and dreamed that the hillside gave way in a mighty quake. The house was crushed under falling rocks and the field of yellow grass slipped down into the sea and all that was left was a gaping brown scar in the earth.

In the morning I packed by bags and left. I took the car down the gravel track to the cove and turned onto the coast road. I drove slowly through the sharp curves of bays, not quite wanting to leave the farmhouse behind. The estuary was, in places, as narrow as a river, with hills rising sharply beside it. The sea, shaded by the hills, was a flinty colour. Here and there, the waves were tipped with grimy spume.

After a while, I crossed a bridge and left the estuary. The road straightened. The hills rising beside it were softer, a lighter, brighter green. I passed a wide sea basin where yachts at their moorings rose and fell on the tide's breath. Before long, I had left the sea behind. The road joined a motorway which ran between lines of hills. Tall, pale cliffs rose on either side. I changed gears and pushed my foot down on the accelerator, speeding past a rumbling van. I felt exhilarated, as if I had just woken after a long and refreshing sleep. The farmhouse now seemed a distant memory, the woman part of a dream.

I rounded a bend and saw the broad, bright sweep of the harbour, its surface turquoise, tiger-striped where the sun broke through pale clouds. Rising at its edges, just as I remembered them, were sharp folds of land, from which houses sprouted at strange angles, as if they had grown wild, and directly ahead of me was the triangle of city buildings, like planted shards of glass.

I felt an urgent need to see Amy. I wished for the smell of her hair and the touch of her fingers on my skin. I wanted to wake beside her, to sit with her at the small pine table in the kitchen as we ate our breakfast, to work at my desk while she watched television or read in another room. As I drove beside the harbour, towards the city's muddle of buildings, I realised how much I had missed those small domestic moments, and I wondered why I had stayed away for so long. But when I arrived at the house she was not there and when I tried my keys in the doors they did not fit. I peered in the window and saw that some of my things—a picture of a man and a woman sitting in a field of maize, their backs blurs of colour against the bright gold, and a statue I had bought once on a trip overseas, of a man curled up on the ground —were gone.

Later, in the library, I began writing a note to her, but all I could think to say was 'I'm sorry.' So I wrote just that. I signed my name and put the note in an envelope, intending to deliver it the next day.

When I had done that I went around the shelves and gathered up some books. I took them back to my seat, which was beside a window, looking out onto a cobbled courtyard. I flicked through some of the books, but soon I put them aside. I think I dozed in the seat because when I next looked up the sun had gone down. I picked up one of the books, an ancient and tatty volume called *Strange Tales* which I had taken from the shelf on an impulse, reaching out to it automatically as I returned to my seat. I suppose I chose it for light relief, but when I opened it my heart leapt into my throat. There, in a book written more than 60 years ago, was a picture of the woman from the farmhouse. It was a casual sketch, an outline rendered in black ink, but I was not mistaken—it was her. For several moments I could do nothing but stare at the picture. I can't recall what I thought during those moments—they are a kind of limbo to me. But after that lost time I flicked back to the beginning of the chapter and read 'The Sad, True Story of The Farmer's Wife.' It lasted only a few pages:

In the spring of 1845, Mr Jacob McClure, of Carlisle, England, and Miss Emily Grant, the daughter of Mr and Mrs Stephen Grant, a parson and his wife, of Scarborough, were introduced on board the brig *Toby*. McClure had purchased some land which he believed would make him a fine farm, and he was furthermore in appearance a strong, steady working man, so, when he made an offer of marriage, Miss Grant quickly assented. They were married on board the *Toby* by the captain, a Scotsman, Edward Wallace, and shortly after arrival in the new settlement they purchased a small boat and made the trip north to McClure's land, which was accessible only by sea. Upon arrival McClure discovered, to his dismay, that the land did not comprise the steady, rolling grassed hillsides he had been promised, but steep, inhospitable hills, densely covered with native bush.

Over a period of years (the exact timing is not known) McClure cleared the land, some hundred acres, one field at a time. As he cleared each field, he purchased a hundred or so head of sheep, which arrived by boat and had to be herded up a narrow gully. He sold most of the timber he had felled and used the rest to build a fine home, which still stands proudly overlooking the inlet. Due to its remote location and challenging terrain, the farm was always marginal. Even after the appearance of a coastal road, which allowed wool to be transported more easily into the city, McClure was year upon year forced to eat into his capital to buy provisions. Sadly, soon after he had broken in the land, McClure perished, falling down a cliff onto rocks abutting the sea inlet far below. He had been trying to repair a fence along the line of the cliff.

After McClure was buried, his wife remained on the farm and managed its affairs while the manual work was done by hired labourers. After some months, sick with grief, she, too, perished on the rocks which had claimed him. The farm lay idle for some months, then passed through several pairs of hands in quick succession. In 1899—forty years after the deaths of McClure and his wife—it was purchased by one William McBride, the son of a wealthy London merchant, who had come to New Zealand on a speculative venture two years previously. It is to McBride's journal that we owe this record. Early on the morning after his first night in the farmhouse he was woken by noises coming from the drawing room downstairs. After he had dressed quickly, McBride went to investigate and found a woman seated in one of his chairs. When he asked her who she was and what she was doing she gave no reply.

'When I entered the room she did not so much as glance in my direction,' he wrote. 'She stared down at her lap as if something there was causing her horror.'

McBride described the woman as bring 'tall and slender, and covered from head to foot in funereal garb'. She was 'quite pale, with a rather narrow face, a small, slender nose and a small mouth more white than red—she might have been quite plain but for her eyes, which were the deep brown of stream water, and were glassy because they were filled with tears.'

Though she left almost straight away, the woman reappeared the following morning at the same time. Again he found her sitting in a chair in the drawing room, staring at her lap with eyes filled with tears.

McBride recounted many mornings after that, in which the woman appeared and sat in the living room. Several times he tried to comfort her, but she rebuffed his attempts either with silence or by standing haughtily and walking out of the house's living room, down the hall and into the kitchen, from where, it seemed, she disappeared.

McBride found that he developed something of a passion for the woman and before long he was spending all of his waking hours sitting with her, watching her, in silence.

After many weeks, one morning she raised her eyes to him and asked him his name. Gradually, over several days, he told her all of his life's story, from his time as a child in London to his voyage to New Zealand and his fortunes since, which had left him a wealthy man. She smiled and listened intently, and he believed he had broken through her wall of silence, 'but when I asked a little of her, again she cast her eyes downward and refused to speak. Yet, so far from being vexed, I was bewitched by this mysterious creature.'

McBride then describes a day in which the woman invited him for a walk around the farm, and as they walked she described for him some of its details, such as the particular rise where the timber for the house had been felled.

'That evening was the most painful of my life,' McBride wrote. 'After we had returned to the homestead and she had settled into her usual position in the drawing room and I had lit a fire in the grate, I knelt before her and pledged my love for her and offered my hand in marriage. She— cruel fate—laughed out loud at the proposition, and said it was far too late for that. She told me, also, that I should forget her and forget that I had ever known her, for she did not love me, and, even if she had, nothing good could ever come of it. Though I protested, she would hear no argument. She simply stood, as she had so many times, and went out the door.

'I did not follow her, for I sensed, though I knew not how, that what had just passed between us were the final words of our affair. I did not expect to see her again, and I did not. Soon afterwards, I was preparing to leave the house—it had become a source of pain—when I came across a drawing which caused my heart to almost leap out of my mouth. It was the woman I had just attempted to wed—I could not be accused of mistaking her—and it bore the inscription *Mrs Emily McClure, 1858*.'

McBride's account is dated August 16, 1900. The District Court records the death of Mrs Emily McClure (nee Grant) 'after falling from a cliff on to rocks below' as August 15, 1859.

The Boy Who Breathed Water

A long time ago, in a town beside the ocean, where the evening wind blew so hard it struck people like needles and the morning sun was grey and thin, there lived a boy, who was curious, and his father, who was careworn and had forgotten how to smile. The boy was full of questions like 'why is the wind so hard?' and 'do fish swim upside down?' and 'why don't frogs chirrup?' which he asked in a tone as light as helium and with brightness in his eyes, but his father was tired and could only shrug and raise an eyebrow over his own dull eye and say, in a faint voice, 'Who knows, whatever.'

It was life that made him sad. He worked long hours in a job he loathed, and all through the day in his musty office he missed his son as if a hole had been shot through his heart. When he got home, he was so tired his thoughts were confused and the boy's face reminded him of his long hours of absence. He felt he was a poor father and that his son would grow up to despise him, so he embraced the boy quickly and snuck away to his room, where he cried until his pillow was soaked with tears.

One day, the boy came to him and asked, 'Father, what would make you happy?' The father shrugged and looked at him ruefully and said, 'Who knows, whatever.'

'What would make you smile?' said the boy, and the father said, 'Who knows, whatever.'

The boy went exploring. He walked to the flax swamp at the edge of town and found a bullfrog that chirruped like a bird. He went for a swim in the sea and saw a halibut basking on its back. He also discovered that the daytime wind was light and soft, like the fur of a persian cat, and the afternoon sun was bright and sharp. At night he told his father of his discoveries and his father shrugged and said his usual words.

The boy explored shops and markets and rubbish bins and gutters. He explored beaches and fields and hills. Each evening he presented his father with a new gift. Once it was a shell, amber in colour, marked with a spiral pattern that grew narrower and narrower until, at the shell's centre, it ended in a tiny point as if it had disappeared into infinity. Another time it was a stone that had been polished by stream water until it appeared as smooth as an egg. Once it was a kiss on the cheek with lips still wet from swimming in the sea—but his father did not smile.

Over the years, the boy also forgot how to smile, and by the time he was fourteen he had come to resemble his father, with a face like a brassica because it was so long since it had been used as faces should. When his friends teased him about his sad appearance, he simply shrugged and said, 'Who knows, whatever.' But one night the boy dreamed he had gone swimming in the sea, and when he had swum so deep his lungs were about to burst he took a tiny breath of water. He woke immediately and was amazed to find he was still alive. In the morning he asked, 'Father, is it possible to breathe water?', and his father, who was still in bed and had his eyes peacefully closed, shook his head slowly. 'No,' he said, between snores. 'It is impossible. Anyone who tries it will drown.'

That night, in the dream, the boy dived into the ocean, holding his breath as he went. As he plunged deeper, the air in his lungs expanded until it seemed they were going to burst. He swum to the limits of his pain, then flipped over and looked up. On the sea's surface he saw the moon, cut into hundreds of thin crescents by the choppy water. Casually, he let the air out of his burning lungs and took a breath of water. He held it for a moment, then breathed it out, and took another lungful.

It did not kill him.

He woke in the morning feeling peaceful, and told his father at breakfast: 'Father, it *is* possible to breathe water.'

His father shrugged and said, 'Who knows, whatever.'

That evening, the father found his son coughing in the bathtub because he had tried to take the soapy water into his lungs and it did not go down like the cool water of his dream. 'Silly boy,' said the father. 'I told you not to.' But in the corner of his eye something glinted.

The boy kept having the dream, and each day he tried again. He breathed from a slimy pond in a vacant section at the end of his street and coughed up algae and mud. He breathed from the swimming pool at his school and his skin turned green. He inhaled seawater and caked his lungs with salt. Then one day he forgot himself during a rainstorm and tipped his head back and drew in the soft clear water in and out as if that was the most natural thing in the world. From then on, he breathed water at every opportunity. He dived into the harbour and took deep breaths which struck him like ice. He breathed the water from streams, rivers, gutters and taps. Before long, he grew happy again and started to smile, but when he spoke to his father of happiness his father said his usual words.

The boy would not give up. Every day he went to his father and asked him to try, and every day his father shrugged. The boy tried to trick his father. One night, as his father slept in a chair in front of television, the boy tipped water into his open mouth, but the water spilled out and ran down his shirt and he woke, spluttering. Another time, he asked his father to come with him to the sea. He waited until his father had waded deep into the water, then leapt on to his back and took hold of his head and forced it into the water. He watched for minutes as the air drained in bubbles from his father's mouth, but his father wouldn't breathe the water and before long he shrugged his son off and waded back to shore.

Nothing worked, until one day a mystical storm blew in from the sea. Its clouds formed a great black canopy over the town and bit by bit dissolved into a shower of silver rain. It came down so hard that the sea overflowed and the streets were flooded to a depth of three feet. Trees drowned. Shops were closed. Everyone was sent home from work and school. But the boy stood in the flooded streets with his face heavenward and his tongue hanging out. Each droplet entered his mouth so softly he felt as if he was swallowing light. The boy cupped his hands and allowed the rain to fill them. He carried the water to his father, who took a small, tentative sip, and smiled at its sweet taste, and then took the deepest, hardest breath he could.

From that day on, neither father nor son could keep themselves from smiling at the merest provocation. The father spent his working hours in a daydream, and the son breathed so much water he could make a person smile simply by whispering their name. After a few years it was forgotten that the father never used to smile, and he and his beloved son became known as the happiest people who ever lived on land. They continued to breathe water for the rest of their lives, and shared their secret at every opportunity, though they were generally not believed.

About the Author

Bernard Steeds is a fiction writer, journalist and researcher from Wellington, New Zealand. His stories have twice won the *Sunday Star-Times* short story competition, have won the *At the Bay* Katherine Mansfield Short Fiction Prize, and been shortlisted or commended in numerous other prizes including The Moth Short Story Prize. His work has appeared in numerous anthologies and journals including *The Penguin New Zealand Anthology: Fifty Stories for Fifty Years in Aotearoa*, and *The Penguin Book of Contemporary New Zealand Short Stories*.

www.bernardsteeds.com